# SECRETS

# SECRETS

## by Fred Steen

## NAVIGATOR BOOKS

# SECRETS

Text Copyright © 2012 by Fred Steen

Cover Photograph Copyright © 2011 by Mark S. Raptis
Used by permission.

## Navigator Books

www.navigator-books.com

ISBN-13: 978-0-9834168-9-0

Printed in the United States of America

I would like to dedicate this book to my dear mother, Willie Lee, and to my wonderful wife, Heidi.

# Acknowledgements

To my beautiful wife, Heidi for, standing by me. To my wonderful enchanted rainbow, Mrs. Maria Edwards, for turning my dream into a reality. I thank Maria for pushing me and believing in me when I had stopped believing in myself. My special thank you to Mr. Ernie Hattery, because Ernie was the point man for our special Infantry rifle company when we walked through the Valley of Death together in Vietnam. We are still friends and Vietnam Brothers, together 44 years later, and Hattery is still the best Point Man since God.

I will always be grateful to Navigator Books for publishing my work, and presenting my work to the public.

I wish to thank my sons, David and Thomas, my granddaughter, Cassandra, and my grandsons Jeremy, Sean, and Adrian. To my dear friends of more than fifty years, Mr. Horace Brooks, Mr. Alvin Norris, Mr. Leonard McKinnon, Mr. Harrel Jones, Mr. Douglas Palmer, Mr. Gene Hudgens, and to Artis and Ollie all the way back to "Down Home." All of my dear friends and family have been an inspiration to me, and to my work.

I thank you one and all.

# "ONE MORE TIME!"

# INTRODUCTION

---

Every one of us are actors and actresses on the universal stages of life. We are dutifully acting out our morally-obligated roles. Those roles are assigned to us by the supreme giver of life and renowned playwright eternal.

In truth, we are assigned our roles at conception—even before birth—where we shout to the world that we are no longer waiting in the wings, that we are now on center stage. *Lights! Camera! Action! Take One!*

There is absolutely no way that we can refuse or alter an assigned role. Make no mistake about it, our parts are given to us for life. Only the firm hand of great Father Death, is empowered by the even greater Playwright, to release us from the parts which we are bound to play. Frankly, it is possible that we are bound to continue playing and acting out our assigned parts, even after death.

It is uncertain to say if one's obligations end with death, due to the cold hard fact that—up to this point in time—no one has crossed the river of death, and returned to say whether or not the play is running on the other side.

To be sure, we often delude ourselves into thinking that we can do it *our* way. That we can say and do something that is not in the script, something that is not in our part. That we can do or say something contrary to what is preordained and written in the script for us to say and do. In that way, we might think that we have actually changed our parts, altered the script, that the outcome is as we made it.

In reality, we haven't changed a thing. The changes that we *thought* we were making had already been written into our parts. In fact, even our mistaken belief that we did things our way was part of the script. Word for word, line for line, every time we are happy, every time we are sad, it is exactly as it is written in our parts.

Some of us are the good guys; some of us are the bad guys; some are only stage and prop hands. Then there are the wardrobe personnel, the makeup people, and of course the musicians and the directors. But even the people behind the curtains are part of the production, each of them acting out their parts, and some waiting for their own moments at center stage.

Some of us continually rehearse our parts, so that we will look and sound good when it is time to perform. We put on the face, and dress like our character is supposed to dress. Most of us have more than one part to play. We find ourselves in a lot of different roles, because—to remain in the play—one must be able to slip into the part of any character that the ever-changing circumstances life may demand.

I am sad to say it, but there are those of us who cannot quickly and easily slip into whatever role our part may call for. Not all of us are capable of acting out every part that the director tells us to assume. Then retribution is swift. We are ordered to leave the stage. We are immediately dropped from the play.

When that happens, our understudy (who is always poised to take our part) is moved in to take over our role. And we are forced into the part of some broken and downcast character on the fringes of the production.

When we turn to the bottle, to drugs, to violence, to murder, those unfortunate choices are already written into our parts. It's all there, written into the script.

Some of us end up playing out our roles in mental institutions, some in jail, in prison, or on the streets—living in

a cardboard box. And *yes*, some of us decide to quit the play…
to get off the stage… to end it all.

And even when we resort to such ends, we are only playing
our parts as they are written. Because what will be, *will be*.
There is nothing that we can do to change that.

It was that very same way with the parts given to Benjamin
and Catherine Marshall, to them and to their parents.

Let's see how well they will play their parts in
*FORBIDDEN FRUIT…*

# FORBIDDEN FRUIT

John and Carina Marshall were excellent parents. Both fully realizing the importance of good parenthood and the family living together, which fostered love and harmony. They were good Christians, steadfast members of the Catholic church, and living proof of that well-known adage—*the family that prays together, stays together*.

Of course, their good family life was destined to be the governing factor in the wonderful characters of John and Carina's two children, a testimony to the loving parents, and to the Marshall family's proud traditions.

John was head of one of the few remaining successful family owned and operated plumbing businesses in the entire city. His personal and business reputation was above reproach, and he was surrounded by satisfied and happy customers.

Carina was a very good and hard-working mother, in the true and purest sense of the word, 'mother.' When the family situation allowed it, she worked in the store with John. However, after the birth of their first baby, she elected to stay home and properly raise their child. Eighteen months later another child arrived, giving them two children to love.

Her reasons for staying home were simple; she wanted be there for her children whenever they needed her. She knew that a working woman who is not home with her kids can also be a good mother, but that was a choice she didn't have to make.

Carina realized that she was fortunate. She didn't have to work. She didn't have to have an outside paying job to make it in her life.

She and John were very fortunate to have their own successful business. She realized that she was blessed, and she vowed to do her very best with the blessings she had been given.

Yes truly, the Marshalls were a well balanced family. Their oldest was a son. His name was Benjamin S. (for Sean), in honor of his uncle, but his family and many friends always just called him, Ben. He was exactly eighteen months older than his sister, Catherine Ann. (Cathy for short.)

The Marshalls were a happy family. Their two children were also happy and well adjusted. They went about their young formative years, growing up in the real world, of good character and of good upbringing. Poised to someday take their places on center stage, as part of the grand play of life, and of death...

It was a time some years ago (or was it just yesterday?) when the lives of the Marshalls, and the lives of those around them, were entwined, one upon the other. All of those near them were very quick and on cue to say, "they are a most wonderful family."

So it was, ever since they were wee tots together, Ben was always very protective of his sister. The first test or example of just how far he would go to protect her occurred when Cathy was around five years old, playing outside in the yard all by herself.

The neighbors had a dog. It wasn't really a bad dog, but rather a *hungry* dog. So when little Cathy refused to share her cookies with the dog, the animal came unraveled and tried to take all the cookies for himself. Of course to make matters worse, Cathy tried to run away, and the dog decided to chase her.

Enter Ben! He saw what was happening, and—with no hesitation—he jumped between his sister and the dog. The dog bit Ben. However, his sister was unscathed.

Their mother saw the incident, and was rushing to help, but Ben was a lot faster. It was a very brave and loving thing for a young boy to do for his little sister.

Years later, when Cathy was an early thirteen and they were both in the same school, the local bully had the hots for Cathy. She wouldn't have a thing to do with him, so—whenever possible—the kid gave her a hard time.

Ben admitted right up front that he was afraid of the bully, who was a big bad guy with lots of muscles, and always had his entourage of supporting bullies with him wherever he went.

One day, when the bully was showing off and pushing Cathy around, he actually made the mistake of slapping her in the face, right in front of her 'wimp' brother.

Well, that did it, 'cause Ben flew into the big bully and kicked his butt all over the school playground. Why, Ben even punched out two of the bully's best supporters. Laid the bully up in the hospital for a whole week, busted him up real nice like.

And all that was done in the actual presence of more than fifty percent of the school's student body.

The principal hadn't a leg to stand on, as far as punishing Ben went. Nearly half the kids in the school had watched the events leading up to the fight. There was no doubt that Ben had been defending his little sister against attack. It hadn't really been a fight anyway, but more of an old-fashioned butt kicking.

Well they all agreed that what Ben deserved was some kind of an award, rather than punishment. The boy was a school hero to most of the students.

To his little sister Cathy, big brother Ben was her very own knight in shining armor. (Without the great steed, of course.)

She would always remember that eventful day, seeing Ben's face as it registered pain when the bully struck her, and then pure rage when Ben attacked the bigger kid.

Cathy grew into a very pretty girl, with most of her beauty emitting from the inside, and her wonderful character making her simple loveliness into something extraordinary. Added to that, she was very smart, a straight-A student, on the Honor Roll, with lots of prestigious awards and honors. If she continued that way, she would go far.

Oh it was she who would help Ben with his homework, and in that way she helped him to achieve better grades.

One could say that Cathy was also very protective of Ben, because she would never sit still if anyone made any derogatory remarks about her brother. They were always very close like that, and a lot of mothers and fathers with sons and daughters, wished their kids were even nearly as close as Ben and Cathy were. It surely did make for a lot of peace and quiet in the Marshall household.

Cathy's plans for her future were not clear, because she was torn between going to medical school, or becoming a nun, a missionary. Her role model was Sister, Saint Cabrini, Frances Xavier (1850-1917), Founder of the Missionary Sisters of the Sacred Heart of Jesus in 1889.

She wanted to enter the Holy Order first, and attend medical school along with her mission in life, so as not to lose any precious time.

Cathy was always very sad when she saw all the misery, pain, suffering and death in Africa, she wanted badly to go there, and to help. Their mother's brother, Uncle Sean, was a Jesuit Priest, already in Africa.

And Ben? Well, it goes without saying, it was very well understood that he would take over the family business, when the time arrived. I guess one could very well say that the Marshall family, was indeed a normal, and well adjusted, average, American family.

Of course everything wasn't always rosy for them, like the time when one of the largest and most popular business customers of theirs suddenly and without warning sued their company. The suit said that John had intentionally installed faulty plumbing in one of their stores, and that faulty plumbing caused an accident which left one of that company's employees unable to work for life.

Of course, the Marshall family stood together in the long and difficult fight to clear their name, and it was plain to all, that time only fused them even more tightly together as a family.

Well anyway, once the case was brought before the courts, it was easily proven that all of the charges were false. Brought on by a company that was in serious financial trouble, and would go under if they had to pay the worker for the accident that their lack of forethought caused. The president of the company confessed, and issued a public apology to John Marshall, his company, and to his family.

That incident took place while Ben and Cathy were in high school.

Sure, it was a victory for John Marshall and family, but you know how people are most of the time. Part of his normal business fell off sharply because of those people who suspected that John really was guilty, and had somehow managed to buy his way out of the lawsuit.

Of course, some of the kids at school thought like their parents, but in the end, even the bad or hard times in the lives of the Marshalls only served to strengthen their family ties.

Ben and Cathy had about the same kind of high school days as the average high school boys and girls were having all over America.

It was somewhere before the time in their lives, when they were confronted with the advent of the birds and the bees. Or when put another way, the time of reckoning and understanding one of the calls of nature, in specific regards, to the desire for sex.

Of course there would be courses, classes, and discussions, all related to sex offered by the school, and I might add, all of those blocks of instruction were excellent, and presented by professionals.

However, Carina and John knew that the final responsibility lay with them because they were Ben and Cathy's mother and father. So it was that, first Ben and his father, had a long honest, and very frank talk regarding sex, and at about the same time Carina and Cathy were having about the same kind of frank bottom line talk.

Later, in keeping with their honored tradition of a family discussion, they all sat together and spoke openly about the same subject. About sex. Both Ben and Cathy knew for sure, that they could come to their father and, ask questions and receive prompt no-nonsense answers.

One of the most important points made during all of the discussions, was the absolute fact, that their school friends, buddies and gals, didn't know any more about the facts of life, about sex, than they knew. That it was sheer stupidity to go and ask one of their friends about sex, or sexual intercourse, when that friend probably knew even less than they knew.

Sure, they each had friends who had already 'done the thing!' But did that make them an expert? Did it suddenly put them in a position of being well versed in the fine art of sexual intercourse? No.

Of course, there was the ever-present fact, that Cathy really did want to become a nun, and she didn't have any intentions of becoming pregnant, and losing her dream, her lifetime desire. And all because of losing control, and not being able to distinguish the difference between her desires and her needs.

Ben was a strong-minded young fellow, and both he and his sister clearly understood the world of differences between love, sex, desire, and need. That's why both the Marshall kids, grew into well-controlled young people. In firm control of their lives...

Sure, they each had a 'special friend,' whom they spent a lot of time with. And those were real friends, because they didn't try and talk Ben or Cathy into doing something that was against their will. Well, at least Ben's girlfriend was a true friend.

Ben's best gal was very pretty, and in some ways she often reminded people of his sister Cathy. Actually, Ben and Harriet Wilson, were friends since their junior high school years. When it was the right time, he gave her his school pin, and she gave him a like token of their relationship, to carry with him. Most of their friends honestly believed that sometime in the future, Ben and Harriet would tie the knot. Because she and Ben were so dedicated to their goals in life, and seemed to be in control, most of their friends thought they would wait until after college to tie the knot. Cause that would be just like them to do so.

Because it was so much like life in the real world, Cathy chose a young man who was *not* like Ben and Harriet, I mean in control. Sure, Darren Lucas was a well bred young man from a good family, and all the other good looking stuff. Darren was hanging on to Cathy in the real hope that someday real soon he would be able to wear her down, and she would give it up, and go all the way down. Cause you see, by that time, Cathy Marshall was one hell of a fine-looking woman. Sure, she was still a teenager. But, in a great difference to her age, her body had matured far past the adolescent stages.

Cathy had an abundance of the very same attributes that men of all ages, 6 to 106 are always looking for in a woman.

Cathy had a magnificently beautiful, full, womanly body. Pretty legs, full perfectly rounded hips, and breasts so outstanding that she was the envy of most of the girls in her class. It was good for her that she was wise enough not to flaunt what she had. Instead, often she deliberately wore clothes that would hide her God-given, womanly beauty.

Now on the other hand, Darren was well aware of what she had, and to tell the truth, he wanted it in the worst old way, wanted to sample her 'box of Cherries.' Don't get me wrong, he wasn't a bad fellow, he just didn't understand the difference between his desires and his needs.

Sure, he understood enough to *pretend* that he understood. A long time before, and many times thereafter, Cathy told him of her dreams, that she wanted to be a nun. And he was smart enough, not to tell her that—in his honest opinion—her becoming a nun would be one of the world's greatest tragedies. Especially after he took her to the beach that first time, saw her in her very conservative bathing suit, and almost had to throw up, 'cause his stomach was all knotted with pure desire. (Or was it pure lust?)

Darren figured that if he could say all the right things, and hold on long enough, someday she would weaken enough and give him what he wanted more than anything in the world. And that was Cathy's body; he wanted to have sex with her. Matter of fact, having sex with her, had clearly become an obsession with him. Plain and simple as that...

It was during the last year of high school, and those years of growing-up had been good to Ben and Cathy. She was the editor of the school paper, and no, Ben wasn't a Saturday evening football hero, but he was still very much liked by his peers and most of the girls in the graduating class.

You see by that last year, most of the upcoming graduating class were fortunate enough to grow up past the quickie in the back seat of a car, a beer when mom and dad wasn't home, or thinking to marry someone, 'cause he or she was a good dancer.

Some of the girls were forced to drop out of school because they got caught pregnant. And some of the boys dropped out of school 'cause the grass seemed greener on the other side.

Some of the girls were wise enough to see Ben for what he appeared to be, a steady young man with his feet on the ground. Going to college, and returning to take over his father's successful business. It didn't matter if he was a poor dancer and it was rumored that he was still a Cherry boy. To dance and to become a good lover, were skills that were teachable. Most of the girls were still plain old envious of Harriet, 'cause she wasn't letting go. Face it, Harriet knew full well when she had a hold of a good thing.

Father O'Brien was very helpful in making the arrangements for Cathy. He was their pastor for almost half of Cathy's life, and took a lot of pride in the fact that she held up and was fully qualified to join a Religious Order. Everything was approved, and it was only a matter of time before Cathy went off to the convent.

The convent was happily looking forward to her arrival. Everyone was proud and happy, that is if you didn't count Darren. Oh that poor fellow was truly heartbroken. He knew that if he didn't finally score before school was out, Cathy would be locked away from him for life. Now that wasn't a very nice prospect, according to the way he was looking at the situation.

One day during that last year, it was Harriet who called Ben's attention to the fact that his sister was positively a most beautiful young woman. And Ben looked at his sister from another angle. For the first time, he saw her for what she truly was, a stunningly beautiful young woman. He could understand why so many of his friends asked him if he could arrange for them to meet his dream of a sister.

He stopped thinking of her as his little sister. She was no longer *little*. In fact, she was full blown. Much, much more than Harriet ever dared to be.

Ben was proud of his sister, that she had stuck by her convictions, that she would soon become a nun, a Catholic Sister of the Cloth. No wonder he had always loved her so very much.

Oh boy was he proud of her, and watching her move gracefully around the house, his love for her grew and grew by huge leaps and bounds. That was one of the reasons that he set aside a time to have a heart-to-heart talk with Darren.

Because the word was filtering back to Ben that Darren was doing a lot of fat mouthing, about him screwing Cathy and how good she was. Darren was telling all his friends that Cathy was a good lay, and that he'd been banging her for quite some time.

It was hard for Ben to accept that Darren was bad mouthing his sister, because he and Darren were pretty good friends, and had been for years.

Cathy said that she had never had sex with Darren or anyone else, that she was still a virgin, and planned to stay that way. Especially, in keeping with her becoming a nun. And Ben believed her, because she had always been truthful to him, and him to her. The bottom line was very clear, Cathy was his little sister, and—even though Darren was her boyfriend, and was a friend to Ben—Cathy was his sister, and Darren had no right to go around spreading lies about her.

Ben didn't want to confront Darren until he was absolutely sure the rumors were true, so he waited, remembering the time he lost it, and beat another boy up real bad. Then one day in the boys room, he actually overheard Darren laughing and telling two other boys how he screwed Cathy only the night before.

Ben knew it to be a lie, seeing as how Cathy was at home with him doing homework, at the same time Darren said that he was screwing her.

Sure, Ben tried real hard to understand Darren's frustration, and his out-and-out lying. Ben tried not to get angry, but just to talk to Darren, man to man. He would only forewarn Darren of the possibilities of a fat lip if he didn't stop lying about Cathy. That's what Ben was planning, when he stepped out so Darren could see that he had been overheard.

However, in the short distance required for him to stand facing Darren, Ben lost it. He proceeded to put Darren's lights out, in addition to busting Darren two fat lips. Ben wiped the floor, using Darren as a mop. Before the other boys managed to pull him off Darren, Ben did Darren a *job*.

Darren found himself in the Aid Station, and of course Ben was in to see the principal again. However, like it was before, there were many students who made it known that Darren had it coming, that he deserved what he got. And the principal was faced with the same situation as before.

That situation was on the bottom of the list of Ben's worries, 'cause he was coming to grips with the major problems within himself. And those problems really worried him a lot.

You see, Ben was very frank with himself when he admitted that it was frightening to him, how quickly and easily he lost his cool. And most of all, the fact that he had come very close to really hurting Darren. Fact was, he had wanted to *kill* him!

If Ben had held a knife, the familiar *blunt instrument*, or (even better) a gun, Darren would not be breathing. There was no mistaking it, Ben was that angry. He was mad enough to take Darren's life!

Ben was haunted by the big question. *Why* was he angry enough to kill Darren?

Losing control that easily was not like him. But even now he was thinking about his dad's gun at home. It wouldn't be all that hard for Ben to get his hands on it…

But he couldn't understand why was he even thinking such a thought. Sure, Darren had acted like a jerk, but it wasn't worth killing him for. Ben was actually shaking in fear with the thought. It was frightening as hell.

He tried to come to grips with why he wanted to kill Darren, but the 'why' eluded him. Or was it that he *saw* the why, and simply didn't want to believe it?

However he did admit that, if the other boys hadn't pulled him off Darren, he definitely would have done some serious bodily damage to the young man.

Yes, Darren was wrong. Yes, the bad things he said might have caused Cathy some embarrassment or problems in her desires to become a nun. Yes, she was his little sister. And because he was her brother, it was his place to stand up for her, to fight for her honor, 'cause that's what big brothers are suppose to do.

But to become angry enough to kill a friend? Now that was the big question.

Sure Darren was just shooting off his mouth, trying to appear big in the eyes of his friends. It was just him bragging, and not thinking how his words were hurting Cathy. 'Cause that old saying that "words will never hurt me" is all a lie.

Of course, the news of the fight, (or rather, the beating) spread like a wild brush fire. Cathy came immediately to Ben's side, even though she didn't agree with what he had done.

She had heard about what Darren was saying around school, but she had chosen to ignore it. She really was almost a nun in her approach to life.

Darren apologized for his unthinking behavior, and even asked the principal not to punish Ben.

John and Carina were very disappointed and shocked when they heard about the incident. But they were not as shocked as

Ben was, when he began coming to grips with what he done. The memories were disturbing. Ben clearly remembered yelling at Darren, primarily for saying that he had screwed Cathy.

"No! You bastard, my God, no! She wouldn't. She couldn't. She's mine. My… my… sister. She's mi…"

His father tried to get him to talk about it, man-to-man. And his mother, being a good mother, and knowing when something was troubling her son also gave it a shot, but with the same results his father received. Ben wouldn't talk about it.

Even when Cathy tried, she received the same end results. Now, Ben felt safe in thinking that, he didn't tell them why he went off like he did, because he really didn't know himself.

Of course, you can probably remember at least one time that you did the same thing. When you lied even to yourself, because it was more convenient than the truth. Sure Ben wasn't positive about the reasons he wanted to kill Darren. But he was as positive as positive can be, at the time he was kicking Darren's butt, that he really wanted to kill him.

Ben went to confession, and his sins were heard by none other than Father O'Brien.

After hearing Ben out, the Father cautioned him about losing his temper. About being over protective regarding his sister, and the fact that she was a young woman, and would someday have to face life's tribulations on her own, and that this problem with Darren had been a good time for her to begin.

Sure they were still in school, but they were also young men and young women, even if they hadn't reached the magic legal ages of 21 and 18.

Father O'Brien had a lot to say about Ben's desire to kill Darren. He made Ben promise that he would come to him, if he ever felt the urge again, *before* he confronted the person that he was angry with.

Ben had been a good Catholic for all of his young life. He had even been an altar boy. Well, Ben failed to tell Father O'Brien what he suspected as his real reason for thinking about dusting Darren.

He also failed to tell the Father about what he yelled at Darren while he was punching the boy's lights out.

After all, Cathy had only one brother, and he had only one sister. He loved her, and she loved him. They were brother and sister, flesh and blood related. And you know the old saying... *Blood is thicker than water.*

No matter how old she was, or what the circumstances, God help the man who hurt her. God help the man who...

The incident was quickly overshadowed with all the excitement of the rapidly approaching end of school for the graduating class. There were still some very important tests to be administered, the school year book's final approval, the rings, and a lot of other things to keep focused on. And even at that early time, there was a lot of buzzing about who was going to the prom with who. And since the beating, Darren had remained unusually quiet and out of sight whenever possible.

Cathy was very wise for her age, and quite frankly, she was worried about Darren and her brother. She saw the look in her brother's eyes when she saw him immediately after the fight. And she saw the look in Darren's eyes.

Ben had really did the poor boy a job, closed both eyes, busted his lips, and even more than the physical damage to Darren, was the fact that Ben came out of it without a scratch.

You know, it's a fact... You can punch a man in the mouth, and not hurt him as much as lightly slapping his face. It has to do with manhood.

So if Ben had been even a little scratched-up, maybe with a black eye, or even just a little blood, it wouldn't have been so bad. Truth was, Darren had his butt kicked, and I do think that was a very fair assessment. Everyone else did, including Darren.

Don't try to fool yourself, sure Darren apologized, and he even apologized to Cathy in front of some friends. Yes, his apology did in some way, lift him up a bit in height to the class and their friends. But, was it *enough*?

Cathy was keenly aware of the great turmoil going on inside both Ben and Darren. To be sure, she knew of the place where her father kept his gun. And because Darren was given to talking a lot, she knew that his father also had a gun, and that gun was readily available to Darren.

One day she even suggested to Ben that he should apologize to Darren, in public, like when he whipped him. Strangely enough, Ben welcomed the idea, and when she told Darren that Ben wanted to see and apologize to him, Darren seemed overcome with joy.

It was Prom Night and the whole world was aglow. It seemed there was a certain enchantment come down upon every member of the graduating class. Oh, Cathy was unanimously voted Valedictorian, and Ben the person who would most assuredly succeed.

Because of Cathy having forethought, there was peace between Ben and Darren. Why, it was Darren who was her escort to the Prom. Matter of fact, Ben and Harriet went along in the car with Cathy, and Darren driving.

Oh I tell you, it was supposed to be a one-in-a-thousand night. Some of those girls who had been holding out would finally consent, and some of the girls who had already done the thing would do it again. With more gusto, and the Devil may care.

They were standing by the punch bowls. (Someone had already spiked the punch to the max.) And that's when Ben took a good look at his sister. 'Cause it seemed that all the other boys were looking so hard, there had already been three fights over that fact.

Yes, oh God yes, Cathy was indeed the belle of the ball. She was stunningly beautiful, looking like a famous movie star at the Academy Awards.

Ben had never seen her so beautiful, that little sister of his.

Darren suggested they change partners for the next dance. Actually, it was the very first time that he and Cathy had ever danced, formally.

She was an excellent dancer, and holding onto her, Ben could not only see what the other boys saw, but he had the advantage of actually *feeling* what they saw. And that was so much, that even he—her brother—was having a tough time dealing with it.

Catherine Marshall was so beautiful. She was a Girl Woman, a Woman Girl, and Ben could easily understand what everyone was looking at. God! He was so proud of her, of his little sister. She was so special to him, and he loved her so much. She would indeed make a most wonderful wife for some very fortunate man one day.

Then he thought, 'No! That won't happen, Cause she's going to be a nun.' And he couldn't help feeling sorry. Sorry for her, for the lucky man who wouldn't have her. Or was he feeling sorry for himself, that he would no longer have a little sister to fuss over and to protect?

Oh, in case you are wondering, Ben and Cathy were able to graduate at the same time, without respect to the difference in their age. Because Cathy was very smart in school, and she was more than able to make up the time difference, so they could graduate together.

After the wonderful dance, they went with a group of their friends to one of their old hangouts. But it wasn't too long before certain couples began disappearing, and soon only Ben and Cathy and a few other couples were left.

They took Harriet home first, and Ben kissed her good night, or good morning, according to how you wanted to look at it. Harriet was all cuddly and dreamy when he kissed her, and looking at Ben with half-closed bedroom eyes. She repeated how she loved him, and thanked him for the most wonderful night in her whole life. A night that she would forever hold dear in her mind and in her heart.

Darren brought them home, and Ben gave them the time together to say good night/morning just like he and Harriet had. Still he was surprised when Cathy kissed Darren.

Their parents patiently waited up for them, and when they were in the house, John and Carina came to hug, kiss, and wish their son and daughter all the luck in the world, out there in the real world.

John had a bottle of Dom Perignon Champagne chilled just right, and a glass for each. Cathy didn't normally drink, but she made an exception in this case, they filled their glasses and toasted to the end of one school, and the beginning of another.

Ben was already accepted at Princeton, and of course everything was arranged for Cathy. They each had a few weeks to get themselves in order.

Well the bottle was about half gone, and so was the early morning. Both John and Carina had a full day ahead of them, so once more around with the kisses and hugs, then they were off to grab a wink before the alarm clock went off.

Ben and Cathy volunteered to clean up a bit. They put things away in the kitchen, and were taking a last look around making sure everything was in order for their mother to make breakfast, which would be taking place in little over an hour.

Ben and Cathy both reached to snap the light off at the same instant. She smiled at him, and he saw that strange light in her beautiful eyes, again.

And it just happened, as naturally as sitting down or getting up. They came into each other's arms, their lips crushed together, hard at first, then very gentle. The sweetness of her was mind blowing. Matter of fact, Ben's mind reeled in an unknown, overwhelming ecstasy. He wasn't in time to hold back the low moan that escaped him. He held onto her for dear life. Sure he had kissed girls before, and he was always kissing Harriet, but sweet Jesus! He had never tasted lips so smooth, so warm, so sweet. It was unreal. He could feel himself trembling, like his heart was about to stop beating, when in fact it was running like a jackhammer.

And Cathy, well add up all that I've just tried to say about how Ben was feeling, then triple it, and that would put you in the ball park of how she was feeling. Her moans matched his, but who was listening?

Yes, it was a long kiss. It had not been planned. There had been no visible preliminaries. But neither of them had ever felt that way before. Not *ever*!

It wasn't plain to either of them who broke the kiss. It was plain as the coming day, if the kiss had lasted any longer, someone would have fainted. For a very long moment, an eternity, they stood silent and breathless, staring into each other's eyes in total disbelief.

Both of them silently saying, "No, no! This is not happening to us. We're brother and sister!" While in reality, their pounding hearts, their still-burning lips, and their quivering bodies said, "*Yes*! Great God almighty! It just happened! It just *happened*!"

Cathy made a tiny gasping, whimpering sound that almost choked her. Then she turned and ran upstairs to her room.

That was a lot more than Ben was capable of doing, 'cause his legs were numb. He stood there watching her until she was out of sight. It wasn't clear to him how long he stood there, staring at the place he had last seen her.

Ben heard himself almost like a distant echo, mumbling over and over. "Oh my dear Lord, Sweet Mother of Jesus, what have I done? Was it the champagne? No! Was it the evening, the night, the time, place, and circumstances? No. No. *No*!"

When he was able to move, he was like a man walking in his sleep. He snapped the light off and made it all the way up the stairs to his room where he collapsed, fully clothed, onto his bed, and staring at the ceiling.

In her room, Cathy was doing the same thing, and wiping the mingled tears of joy and disgrace from her eyes.

"I'll just make believe that it didn't happen," she whispered. "Clearly it was the champagne. I'm not used to drinking, and we were carried away by the wonderful evening. After all, we are from a good Catholic family. Oh my God, I must *never* tell Mother, 'cause she would die.

"I can't even tell Father O'Brien. I can't tell anyone, not even God. I just kissed my own brother, and I felt..."

She curled her young luscious body into a fetal position, and silently cried and cried.

But you know what? The sheer joy of that kiss flatly refused to be washed away, no matter how many tears Cathy cried. What was done, was done, and that was a cold hard fact!

In his own room, Ben wasn't crying. He tried to cry, to beg the Good Lord to forgive his sins. But his eyes remained dry. He hoped that crying would give him some small amount of absolution. It didn't.

When the first light of the new day came creeping silently into their rooms both Ben and Cathy were still trying to cope with life. And to be frank about it, they weren't making any headway at all.

They were so much like Sweet Willie and Barbara Allen from the old folk song, because the world wouldn't even *try* to understand.

Carina Marshall went about fixing breakfast as usual. After their long night of celebrating, she really didn't expect her children to join her and John at the table. Surely Ben and Cathy would still be sleeping, and dreaming of the wonderful future lying ahead of them. So she fixed breakfast only for her and John. Ben and Cathy could get their own breakfast.

John was in the process of buying another company, and growing their successful little company into an even larger success. Carina was responsible for checking the other company's books, and she would be spending the next two weeks away from home, looking over the finances. She and John worked hard together.

But not to worry... Cathy and Ben would be home. They would take good care of the house, with Cathy preparing all of the meals, with Ben's help of course.

Carina and John were so proud of their children. They were really a bit saddened by the fact that in a short time, Ben and Cathy would be out of the house. Away from home, off to college and to the convent. She and John had raised their children in a good loving home, and in the church. They would be all right, and more than able to cope with life.

After breakfast, Carina thought to check on Cathy, because Cathy had an appointment to see Father O'Brien. She decided to call later from the office to remind Cathy, just in case she might forget. So John and Carina left the house quietly in an effort not to wake their sleeping children.

In truth, there was no need to worry about waking them, because you see, they were not asleep. Sleep had avoided both of them like they had the plague.

Ben was having a bowl of cereal when Cathy came into the kitchen. It seemed that both of them had somehow come to the same conclusion regarding their kiss. It was best to just ignore the whole thing, pretend that it had never happened. It had been an accident. That was all. Better to just walk on by, like it had never really happened.

They exchanged friendly greetings, just like always. Cathy asked if Ben slept well. He nodded, and inquired the same of her, receiving the same lie in return. One look at both of their faces told the real truth, her swollen and red eyes, and his eyes looking like two cherries in a glass of buttermilk.

But they were doing a good job of putting up a front. Cathy decided to join her brother in having cereal, because all the makings were right there on the table. They talked about everything possible, avoiding prom night, and the sweetest kiss that either of them had ever experienced.

Sure it was strange, because most of the other kids who were a part of that once in a life time occasion were certainly talking about it.

The conversation between them made no real sense, and they went to great lengths to avoid eye contact. And suddenly, they were staring at each other. In that moment, both Cathy and Ben Marshall knew the truth. It *wasn't* over. The crazy unplanned kiss of the night before had not been the end of it. They stopped their mindless chattering, and looked deep into their almost empty cereal bowls, remembering and trying real hard not to.

The longer they sat there in silence, the louder the silence grew. When Cathy looked up, she stared directly into Ben's eyes, and her stomach did a mad flip.

Ben stared back. He had never realized just how beautiful his sister really was. He tried to drive that thought away, but it kept coming back to him. Cathy was so beautiful…

Without a word, Cathy began clearing the table and putting the used dishes into the dishwasher. Just as silently, Ben began helping her. They were doing the things they had done a thousand times, so no words were required.

The phone rang. It was their mother, reminding Cathy that she had an appointment with Father O'Brien.

Cathy and Ben spoke only when it was absolutely necessary, regarding dinner and a few other things that only required a one-word answer from either of them.

Harriet called first, and as soon as Ben hung up, Darren called. He and Cathy agreed on a meeting place, and about 20 minutes later, she was gone.

Ben's favorite thinking place was in the garage, where there were a lot of old cartons full of stuff from the family business. After Cathy left, he went to the garage, sat in his favorite spot and began to think.

Yes, what he had done was *wrong*. Capital W.R.O.N.G! And no matter how hard he tried, he wasn't able to make himself believe it had been an accident. It really was a mutual thing, because she had kissed him back. She hadn't pushed him away. If her actions, her breathing and trembling were any indication, she had enjoyed the kiss as much as Ben had. Surely it was a mutual thing. No way around it.

Was it simply an overreaction to that wonderful night? Simply two young people who became mixed-up, and carried away, going a little bit too far? Maybe it had just been a little mistaken kiss. Maybe it meant nothing. After all, they were brother and sister.

And everyone knows it's wrong for a brother to feel that kind of attraction for his own sister. A man who would stoop that low should be put away, or better yet, shot!

Was Ben attracted to his own sister? No! No! No! He was screaming 'no' out loud. But in his heart, he was screaming something to the opposite.

"It's not right," he said in a more conversational tone, as he was forced to leave his favorite thinking place, 'cause it hurt too much to think. "Aw forget it. Go pick Harriet up, and take her for a ride. Perhaps being with her will clear your head."

When Cathy arrived for the meeting, Father O'Brien wasn't there. He had been called to an emergency, so Cathy went into the church and sat near the statue of the Virgin Mary. That was *her* favorite thinking place.

She had a more realistic approach to the matter. Yes! She had wanted Ben to kiss her for a long time. The kiss in the kitchen had not been an accident.

No, she hadn't planned it that way, but when it happened, she'd had the time to push him away, to avoid it. But she hadn't.

Yes, she was excited beyond words. Yes, she was sorry that it had happened. Yes, it was wrong, but she would not go to confession and confess her sins.

Her feelings for her own brother were wrong, against the teachings of the church. It was a great sin that would really hurt mother and father, no doubt about that.

She decided to avoid Ben until things cooled down, and she promised the Virgin Mary (and herself) that she would make sure that it never happened again. Not *ever*.

When Father O'Brien returned, they spoke of the final arrangements, and he told her that Mother Superior, the Reverend Mother Segovia, was looking forward to seeing her.

Later, when Cathy was on her way back home to start dinner, it struck her real hard, and for the very first time... Would it be *right* for her to go to the convent, after what had happened? She should have gone to confession. She hadn't. She should have pushed Ben away. She hadn't.

Deep down in her heart, her feelings for him were definitely not right. Should she continue on with her dream? Or should she *not* go to the convent?

Oh it was very hard for her. What if she suddenly changed her mind, after all those years? After a lifetime? Her mother and father didn't deserve to be punished for her wrongdoing, for her lack of discretion. Oh what to do?

It seemed the only thing to do was to avoid Ben, and make sure they never kissed again.

Of course it was only a few days later, when they were all alone, her mother suddenly asked, "Honey, what's up between you and your brother? You two are most definitely avoiding each other. Yet, I catch you looking longingly at him, when he is not looking. And I catch him doing the same thing. What happened? Did you two have a fight?"

"We were trying to decide about whether we should have a going away party," Cathy said. "And where we should have it. We agreed not to try and influence each other's decision."

Cathy felt the weight of the lie immediately. She had just pulled the answer out of thin air. It was so lame that she could hardly believe her mother bought it. Cathy was both relieved and ashamed. She almost blurted out the truth.

A week and a half passed, and they had to start talking to each other again. Their father noticed the silence between his children, and asked what was wrong.

In the end, it was easier for all concerned if Ben and Cathy carried on as usual. After all, it had only been an unthinking kiss. Sure, it was wrong. But it was forgivable, as long as they didn't do it again.

Ben came to borrow Cathy's copy of the latest number one song. She held onto it, until he promised not to keep it more than an hour. Ben playfully grabbed for it, and caught her instead.

Now that time, it was most deliberate because they stood there staring at each other for a full minute before Cathy came slowly and most deliberately into Ben's arms. They stared into each other's eyes for a long time. Then, they put their quivering lips together in a warm, tender, and most passionate lovers' kiss.

This time, there was no mistaking the intent in either of them.

"Cathy, I love you with all my heart," Ben said between the second and the third kiss. Or was it between the *third* and the *forth*?

Cathy was trying to get her breath, and shook like never before. Because she loved him too, and she whispered those same words to him. "Ben oh Ben, I love you too. Oh my dear God, I know it's wrong, before man and before God. But Ben, I love you."

They stood there holding on to each other, brother and sister locked in a lover's embrace.

"Oh Ben, it's so wrong, it's so very wrong, but I can't help how I truly feel in my heart. I love you. I've loved you since when we were kids."

"Cathy, I know now that I've loved you since that time too. All of my life I've loved you. I wish that you were not my sister, my flesh and my blood. But there's nothing that we can do to change it. No one will understand. In truth, I'm not even sure that *I* understand."

His voice softened. "But I *do* understand that I love you."

"We have to be adults about this," he said. "We must talk, and not hold anything back. Maybe it's because of the fact that we are both inexperienced. That neither of us have actually gone with someone else. Maybe it's because we have been *too* close together, as brother and sister.

"That we really do love each other as brother and sister, and not as lovers. Maybe we are expressing our mutual love for each other in the wrong way, because it is the only way that we know of," he said.

Cathy shook her head. "Ben, you have always been the clear-thinking one. You are not given to doing things on the spur of the moment. You always think things out. That's why Dad says you will do better than he, when you take over the business. Do you really—deep down in your heart—think that our feelings for each other are mistaken? Misunderstood? Nothing more than a childish crush? Do you really think we don't understand love... the love a man feels for a woman?"

She smiled sadly. "And make no mistake about it, we *are* man and woman. We're not kids anymore."

"Okay," Ben said. "I won't touch you. Let's go down to the kitchen, and while we are fixing dinner, lets you and me really talk about how we feel about each other. We won't hold anything back. 'Cause what we say to each other, can come back to haunt us, and to haunt our family and friends forever."

They laid it all out where they could plainly see it, didn't hold back a thing. Told it like it was, like the real and true adults they were. 'Cause, you see, Ben and Cathy had to shuck off the mantels of childhood, of adolescent protection. They had to step boldly out into the real world, and without the support of their mother or father.

Ben and Cathy had tasted the forbidden fruit. They had bitten the apple.

When their talking was through, it was plain that Ben and Cathy actually loved each other, man to a woman, woman to man. And most certainly not, brother to sister, or sister to brother.

Yes, it was all wrong and it should never have happened, But it had happened. It was morally wrong. It was legally wrong. It was physically wrong. But none of those things could change the truth. They really *did* love each other.

The big remaining problem was simply, what to do about it?

Was it better for all concerned that they pretend it never happened? Could they lock their love for each other up tight in their hearts, and keep it a secret for the rest of their lives?

Maybe in time it would go away, and they would be free to go on with their lives. After all, Ben had Harriet. She loved him and would make him a very good wife. Cathy would have her life as a nun, helping the poor and the needy. Doing missionary work for God.

Their secret need never be told.

Cathy and Ben carried on their lives as expected, proceeding towards the day when he would leave for college, and she to the convent. In the meantime she continued going out with Darren, and Ben with Harriet.

It was better to live a lie than to hurt the people they loved so much. Their little secret was still hidden.

Sometimes, they would steal away and grab a precious moment of time. Afterwards, they would almost always ask themselves if their love was really true? And the answer was always, *yes*!

Would Cathy lie to God? Would she go into the convent, loving and wanting her own *brother*? Would she take the final oath, before God?

Would Ben actually marry Harriet, and knowing all the time that it was his sister that he really wanted? What would that do to Harriet? Would he be so callous as to destroy her life?

Oh, just in case you are wondering, up to that time, Ben and Cathy had not been to bed together. They hadn't had sex. You see, really and truly, their love for each other was not about sex.

Yes, Harriet would gladly give her body to Ben. She had already said so. And he had already told her that he wanted to wait, not to make sure of her, but to make sure of himself. You see Ben was in reality, a very nice young man.

And the same went for Cathy. Don't forget, they were both very nice young people. Smart, of excellent character, and with an outstanding upbringing before God.

Unfortunately for the two of them, old Fate dealt them a real bad hand, most of their cards coming from the bottom of the deck. Perhaps, if they played their hands right, they could still win the game. What do *you* think?

Life and things continued to run along smoothly for them. Their family business was doing really well, and John was repeating over and over again how happy he would be when Ben was able to step in and help him.

Of course both their mother and father were looking forward to the proud moment when their only daughter would be a full-fledged nun. No doubt about it, they were very proud parents.

Cathy and Ben always felt real guilty, but up to that point in time, no real harm had been done. What was between them was a well-guarded secret. They were very careful to keep it that way, knowing full well if they were ever caught kissing, their world would fall right in on their heads and bury them.

It was only three days before Ben would be off to college, and about five days before Cathy was to leave too. There was a Plumbers Supply Convention taking place in Washington, D.C. John didn't want to go, but, it would be very good business if he and Carina did attend. Besides, they would be home a full day before Ben was due to leave.

So it was a very last minute decision that they were going. When they told Cathy, she seemed unusually different. And because Carina was a good mother, she added that difference to all of the other little differences in her daughter that she had been noticing and filing away. Cathy was keeping something a secret, and her mother wondered what.

Up to that point in time, they'd had an excellent Mother-Daughter relationship. But Carina didn't have time to really talk to her daughter, 'cause there was the packing and getting off to DC.

Oh, she did approach Cathy, but Cathy was getting real good at warding off anything that might unlock her terrible secret. There was a lot of running around to do before they were gone, and Ben and Cathy had that great big house all to themselves.

They tried very hard to avoid each other, bound and determined not to make matters worse. Cathy even tried to spend the night with a friend of hers, but the attempt fell through. They were doing okay. Rather than fix something for dinner, they called out for pizza.

They didn't even kiss, but sat watching TV, and talking about when Ben would be away at college, and some about the time when Cathy thought the bogey man was under her bed, and she ran to sleep with Ben. Their parents called later, and then Cathy and Ben went to their separate bedrooms, to bed.

The house was very quiet, perhaps a little more so in the absence of John and Carina. It was a little more than two hours since Ben and Cathy said good night, Ben's clock radio showed the time to be three minutes to midnight.

Since he came to bed, he was trying unsuccessfully to read again, the tale about the Dancing Men, from the Adventures of Sherlock Holmes. The story was one of his favorites, but for some reason he found it very hard to concentrate on Sherlock Holmes.

"Ben my lad, that would be very wrong," he said to himself. "She is your only sister, and tonight there is no earthly reason or excuse for you to do the things you're thinking about. What would Mom say? And you know that Dad would just kill you, and get it over with. Stop thinking about Cathy! Think about Harriet, or read The Hounds of the Baskerville, 'cause you always like that."

Ben was still talking to himself in a futile attempt to get his mind and heart off of Cathy, when she came into his room.

"Ben," she said shyly, "there's a Bogey Man under my bed."

Ben sighed. "Now that you are here with me, that bad old bogey man will go away," he said. "Come to me little one. I'll protect you, forever and ever."

And Cathy came to Ben.

Oh, it was a time when an age-old *wrong*, was suddenly turned very *right*. When an age-old wrong, literally ceased to *be* wrong. Brother and Sister were no longer brother and sister, creating a void, and in that void rushed the young man and woman.

In a gesture as old as time itself, she came to stand before him, allowing her only garment to fall to the floor, like the fluttering wings of a butterfly.

He sucked in a giant breath of excitement.

Cathy stood there before him, clothed only in her flawless, enchantingly beautiful, pure womanhood.

Yes! It was a sight that he had never before seen. In the name of the supreme being, she was the single most beautiful, the most magnificent breathtaking creature in all the world.

Ben rushed to Cathy, taking his sister into his arms to make her a woman.

She cried out in pain when his body entered hers. She cried for the coming of age, in the pain of her very first time. She cried out in the pure ecstasy of giving and receiving, of partaking of the forbidden fruit. She cried out in the full realization and submission to her greatest desires.

Sometimes, we lose sight of what's right, because we're spending too much time looking at what's wrong. Ben and Cathy forgot about wrong, as they found right in each other's arms.

Together they rode on a bright shining comet, trailing in its wake a million multicolored stars. Riding on that great magical comet, they went surfing across the most distant and far-reaching expanse of the galaxies.

Holding tightly onto each other, sometimes laughing, sometimes crying, their minds reeling and racing right up to the very edge of oblivion. They had to hold tightly to each other's naked, sweating, and trembling bodies. Holding on for dear life to all the love and devotion the Creator had endowed them with.

At one point along the way Ben whispered to Cathy of his great love for her, and in turn, she whispered of her love for him.

Oh, I tell you, it was the time of the Creation. The time of the Genesis and the Apocalypse, of the Alpha and the Omega.

It was the time, when together they screamed, united in a cataclysmic explosion of right and wrong. Of the *bad* that was so damn *good*!

"Ben-O-Ben!"

"Cathy-O-Cathy!"

It was a very long time before they came down from the top of the mountains. Before they regained the capability of speech, and they said to each other, him to her, and her to him... "I love you!"

When they set foot on the 'real world' again, they were wise enough to know that it was again time to talk, to plan, to come to grips with...

Ben said, "Cathy, I love you. I'm asking you to please marry me. We can go to Canada, where we will be unknown, and start a new life for us. I think it's best for all concerned, that we continue on with our plans. So as not to hurt our parents, because they don't deserve the hurt that the knowledge of our love would cause them. Neither will I tell Harriet, I will not hurt her either. Let's you and me go off to our destinations, and when the time is right, we simply disappear. Never to be seen or heard of again."

"Ben I would not be here with you, if I didn't love you. Yes, I'll be your wife. I agree with you on your plan for our future. But, we'll have to make our move before it comes to the point in my life when I must lie to God. Ben, after what we just did, I cannot become a nun.

"In truth, I've given up my dreams to be yours. I know what we've done is totally wrong. But, I love you and in the same breath I beg the Dear Lord to forgive us both.

"Shall we tell Father O'Brien? Because I think he is the only one in all the world who might understand what we've done. I'm going to pray to God for the forgiveness of our sins. But I'm not going to tell Him that I'm sorry for what we did."

She paused. "Ben? Do you think that is wrong? That it will only add to the anger that God may have for us?"

In the Old Testament, in the book of Genesis, Abraham the father had two sons – Isaac and Jacob.

And it is written in Genesis 29:10 — *When Jacob saw Rachel daughter of Laban, his mother's brother. Then Jacob kissed Rachel and began to weep aloud.*

29:14 — *Then Laban said to him, "You are my own flesh and blood." Jacob wanted to marry Rachel first, and worked seven years for her, but was first given Leah, because she was the oldest, he worked another seven years for Rachel.*

29:23 — *And Jacob did so, he finished the week with Leah, and then Laban gave him his daughter Rachel to be his wife. In fact, Jacob married Leah, his mother's brother's daughter, Before he married Rachel the second daughter to his mother's brother. Jacob was married to both women.*

The following morning when they awoke, Ben and Cathy most deliberately looked into each other's faces. They were very wise to do that, 'cause you see, sometimes at night, in the heat of desire, things very often appear different than those same things appear in the light of day.

Did you know that? Well it's very true. Take it from one who's been there before.

Once again, it was time to speak frankly. They agreed to stick to the original plan of continuing with their lives as though nothing had changed. They would bide their time, and wait for the moment when they could run away together. Things would work out fine, as long as their dark secret remained hidden.

The days passed, and finally the day arrived for Ben to leave. His departure was amid more than the usual amount of well wishes, kissing, and hugging.

Before leaving, he had a down to earth, heart-to-heart with Harriet. Yes, it was hard for her to accept, and even harder for her to understand. But Harriet was a real trooper, don't forget that she was really in love with Ben, and had been in love with him for a long time.

Sometimes true love is so hard to define, because there are no limits or boundaries. Think about it.

A few days later, there was a repetition of events in the Marshall household, very much like Ben's departure, except it was Cathy on the receiving end. It was so hard for her to pretend. More than one time she wanted to leap into her mother's arms, to throw herself at the feet of her loving parents, and moan, "Mom and Dad... We have sinned most grievously!"

In truth she felt dirty, lacking appreciation, and very much like a female Judas Iscariot. There she was, kissing and hugging her mother and at the same time she had a foot long dagger in her mother's back. In the back of the woman who had given her life.

She found it almost impossible to look her parents straight in the eye. Oh, that poor child had one hell of a load on her young shoulders, a load that she knew would grow heavier, and heavier as the long days passed. Such were her sins.

When she reached the convent, she found it just as hard to look the Reverend Mother in the eye. Oh, what a time.

She and Ben remained in daily contact, even when the strict rules of her new surroundings made it difficult. The rules were unbending, but Cathy kept her trusty cell phone handy.

The first few days of settling-in were smooth and even pleasant for Cathy, 'cause she did so enjoy the times spent at chapel. It gave her time to talk with God, and still she wasn't ashamed of loving Ben, her brother.

Of course, as time passed, it made it harder and harder for her not to come clean with Mother Superior. She felt more and more that she owed all of them—her parents, Father O'Brien, and the Good Mother—the honest and straightforward truth.

Believe it or not, Cathy really did feel that she had made her peace with the dear Lord.

Well, as it is more often to happen as not to, Old Fate took a hand in the proceedings, and blew everything all to hell. All their best laid plans went up in the smoke.

Yeah, you guessed it! Cathy missed her 'monthly,' missed her 'time' and missed it by a good old country mile. No doubt about it, she was pregnant.

And No! There wasn't the slightest chance that she was wrong.

Now didn't that beat all? Oh, there was no need for her to use one of those pregnancy test kits, which I might add, weren't readily available to her due to her situation at that time. On the other hand, Cathy might have been a sinner, but that didn't mean that she was a fool.

She knew her body, and in that way she knew for sure that she had conceived. She was pregnant, going to become a mother.

Sure she thought about holding on for a while, and not to tell Ben. To begin hoping for a miracle that she was smart enough to know would not be coming. That there was absolutely nothing to be gained from her delaying letting him know. So she told him right away, and in some ways was happy when he didn't question her.

Instead, he said right away, "Cathy, don't you worry. I'll protect you. We can no longer delay the unavoidable."

Just like always, Ben was right. Old Fate was at it again, and forcing her to show her cards or to throw her hand in. It was way past the time for her to shed some of the terrible load that was dragging her all the way down to the ground. So she requested permission to see Mother Segovia.

When she was comfortably seated in the Reverend Mother's office, Cathy laid her soul bare to the bone, and confessed all of their sins. Ending with how truly sorry she was to have knowingly deceived all of the wonderful people who loved her, and whom she loved so dearly.

Cathy begged for the forgiveness of God the Father, her parents, Father O'Brien, and the Reverend Mother sitting there before her. But she truthfully explained that she wasn't sorry. Oh, she was surely ashamed, but *not* sorry for loving Ben, for loving her very own brother. And she wasn't sorry for the child in her womb, of which Ben was surely the father.

After Cathy finished her very emotional and tear-stained confession, Mother Segovia took long moments in meditation before she spoke. She couldn't tell Cathy that this was the first time she'd had to face a sin like that one, or how very sorry she was to hear of it. Or that she was saddened to lose such a wonderful convert, a woman who seemed destined to become a wonderful nun. The Reverend Mother had to get herself together before she spoke. She was hurting too.

"Well, my dear... I thank you so much for coming to me. Of course you already know how I feel about the great sin that you and your brother share, so I'll not even attempt to sit in judgment. I'll not say a word regarding what you have to do, what you have to confess to God our Father.

"Oh my dear, I'm afraid that you are going to be judged rather harshly by those who will come after our Father, and after me. I'll not hold you back from doing what you have to do. I'll not help you, but I will not stop you from going to Ben.

The old nun sighed heavily. "I will talk to Father O'Brien, but my talking to him will not in any way relieve you of your moral responsibility to tell him yourself.

"Cathy, it's you and *only* you who must go to your family, to your mother and father, because they do so deserve to hear the truth, and most of all, to hear it from you and Ben.

"My child, when you first arrived here to begin your training, I could see this in your eyes, even though you tried so hard to hide it. And Cathy, I saw something else. It was something of a blessing in disguise, of God working His divine will in many different ways. A blessing that will come from a mother, to a mother-to-be.

"I will not say anything more at this time. I suggest that you go to chapel, get down on your knees and talk with God the Father. For it is in Him that you will find your *first* salvation."

After that, Mother Segovia appeared very sad, and tried to hide the tears welling up in her old eyes.

Cathy and Ben arranged to meet in one of the local off-campus spots near his college, where they could talk and come up with a plan of action. There were two possibilities. One— they could both go straight home, tell their story and face the music. After all, they never once doubted the fact that their father and mother would hear them out, and not turn their backs, no matter what.

Two—they could take what they had and run for Canada. But they decided that going to another country would usher in a lot of new legal problems. They talked about Las Vegas, Hawaii, or even Alaska.

In the end, they decided on Las Vegas, because Ben knew of some possible connections, people who didn't know Cathy or his parents. Also, the marriage regulations in Vegas were rather relaxed. That would suit them just fine.

Ben had access to enough money to see him through college, so fortunately for them, finances were not a problem.

It wasn't difficult for Cathy to get away, based upon another lie she told her mother, that she would be in seclusion, meditating. That way, Mother Segovia wouldn't be put in the position of telling the truth, when it came right down to it.

Ben had to come up with a tall tale about a family emergency. Of course, if you really looked at it that way, there truly *was* a family emergency. (Or would that be stretching it a bit?)

Anyway, they managed to get away together, and to do it without raising any suspicion. Everyone thought that all was well.

\*     \*     \*

It was one of the finest hotels in Las Vegas. They registered and took rooms there, no questions asked.

Getting married was a bit stickier. The clerk raised an eyebrow concerning the fact that Cathy and Ben both had the same last.

Cathy joked that there was a million-in-one chance that both she and her boyfriend would have the same family name. After all, there were a lot of people with Marshall as their family name. And she laughingly asked if the clerk thought she was marrying her father or her brother?

The clerk smiled at what he thought was her little joke. Obviously it was just a coincidence. Whoever heard of a pretty young girl marrying her own brother?

So Ben and Cathy were legally married. Man and wife, their license issued in the state of Nevada.

Mr. and Mrs. Benjamin Marshall checked out of the hotel one morning and moved into a very nice rented apartment in a well to do neighborhood. Again, no questions asked, especially since Ben had the money.

Three days later he was interviewed for a job, and because of his great knowledge of the plumbing business, he was hired with a very good starting salary.

Two days after that, Cathy was hired as a substitute teacher in a nearby day care center. It was all that easy.

All of their neighbors were very nice people and rushed to accept the new young couple across the street.

In a way, it was something of a coup to the brilliant mind of Ben, with Cathy's support of course. They were brilliant people, and resourceful enough to do all of that in a reasonably short time, without any real prior planning. And no one back in their home town knew one thing about what they did.

Which proved, that one can move mountains with a focused mind. Pretty good, huh?

The highway of life was open to them, all they had to do was look out for the bumps in the road. Cathy wondered if her baby would be, normal, seeing as how the baby's father was also its uncle. Or *was* it?

They enjoyed their new status in life, but their joy was extremely short-lived. 'Cause you see, there was a lot of unfinished business... skeletons in the closet, and they were both troubled by a guilty conscience.

A conscience that flatly refused to go away, and was insistent on haunting them continually. When they were together, they made it a point not to speak of it, although they were both smart enough to know that the problem wouldn't go away.

Cathy was a good Catholic woman, and she was shocked when she thought of suicide. To take her own life and that of the still forming child, in her womb. Chances were very good that she would be doing the child a favor, because the close in-breeding, incest, of her baby's inception might lead to serious birth defects. Could she *do* it?

Cathy wasn't alone in this idea. Ben gave the same awful thought a whirl. He was going to be a very bitter disappointment to his father. Who would take over the family business that his father had soaked his whole life into? How much pain, dishonor, and humiliation, could his parents stand, when their friends, neighbors, and customers pointed and whispered behind their backs. About their son screwing his sister, their daughter.

What he and Cathy had done might be enough to actually kill their parents. Could he *do* it? Could he take his own life?

You know, in the end, it was really their mother and father who saved them from suicide. Ben and Cathy had been raised in church, in a healthy family, strongly bonded with love. That love, strengthened by prayer and understanding, was the foundation that kept their family standing in the storm.

Ben and Kathy thought of Father O'Brien, who—just like their parents—had always been there for them.

So they threw the suicide idea out of their minds. Truth was, regardless to the great sins they had committed, Ben and Cathy loved their parents. They loved their church, their community, and make no doubt about it, Ben and Cathy did love each other.

Sure what they were doing was wrong, but sometimes we can't distinguish the trees from the forest. Especially, when we become wrapped up in ourselves, and forget what we are doing. Check it out.

Of course Ben continued to call home at the normally accepted times, and Cathy snatched the opportunity to call too. They knew better than to rock the boat, or to suddenly do or say something that was out of the ordinary.

They were young and inexperienced in the ways of the world, and yet they were actually doing okay, making things work for them. I hope you are not one of those people who think that brains are based upon age. That one must be *old* to be *smart*, when in-fact, age is nothing but a number.

Ben and Cathy established their very own clandestine world of existence. Sure it was based upon the will and the desire to be together, to buck the system, upon lies. But it worked!

To be sure, it wouldn't last, and they both knew it was just a matter of time before Father O'Brien would place a call to Mother Segovia. Their mother or father would decide to pay them an unsuspected visit, to see how things were going. Or someone from back home would be in Las Vegas, and happen to run into Ben, or see Cathy at the day care center.

What they had was fragile at the most, but so is life itself. One minute we are living, the next minute we are dead. Think about it.

Friday came, the very last of the days that Mother Segovia had promised to cover for them. They had been very lucky up to that point in time. And I hasten to add, very sick of all the lies, covering the lies. It was a very sad and hurtful time, for two young people who had always been raised to speak the truth.

Now that was the time when, they sat facing each other, and silently staring. Words were quite unnecessary, when they suddenly smiled in silent agreement. Ben reached for the phone, dialed a number, spoke briefly to someone, put the phone down. He said to Cathy, "Honey can we be there in 42 minutes?"

"Yes!" she said, already in motion.

It was finally time to do the right thing. Sure, it was a bit late, but you know the old saying... *Better late than never*!

Their mother was still in the kitchen finishing cleaning-up from a late dinner, and their father was down the street to visit Russo, his long time buddy, helping to install a new program on Russo's computer.

Their father was delighted to hear that his son and daughter were home. *What a wonderful surprise... He would be right there.*

At last, they sat at the kitchen table, John, Carina, and their two children. There were two pieces of mom's excellent homemade apple pie left. For a moment, Cathy and Ben felt like they had before they'd left home. They sat, munching the wonderful homemade pie and having a cold glass of milk with it.

Oh, it was so good to have them home, but Carina had an uneasy feeling in the bottom of her stomach. Something wasn't right. She could feel it. After all, she was their mother, and good mothers can always most certainly feel when something is wrong.

Ben and Cathy remembered what their parents had always said... "You can come to us at any time, with any problem. We will *always* listen. No matter what it is, or how big it is, we can handle it together."

So it was that John and Carina listened, just like they had always said that they would. They listened without interruption. They tried to hide the sudden misty eyes, listening and feeling the same emotions their son and daughter were feeling. At one point Carina was openly weeping, and John tried to comfort her in vain.

Oh, I tell you, Cathy and Ben had never before seen their parents so miserable, in so much pain, or their father weeping, before that sad time.

It was the very first time that Cathy felt really and truly sorry that she had fallen in love with Ben. Both she and Ben were so ashamed they were weeping too. They were most grievously ashamed for causing their mother and father so much pain, and knowing at the same time that this was only the start of it—the very first installment. In their community, they would pay. In church, they would pay. In the world, they would pay.

Ben was crying and wringing his hands. When he finally spoke, his voice was a little too loud. "Mom, Dad, it's all my fault. I'm the oldest, and Cathy is my baby sister. I should have known better. But really and truly, I love her more than I love life itself.

"But that fact won't wash away what I did. It was *all* me, all my doing. Please don't blame Cathy. She didn't know better. She didn't *know*…

"Please don't cry, Mom. I'm so sorry. Dad, I… I… I wish that I could undo the damage and the pain that I've caused you both. It's not that I don't love you… Please, let Cathy and me leave you now, before anyone knows that we came. We'll go back to where we came from, quietly disappear, back into our great shame.

"We didn't mean to hurt you so much. We were thinking only of our love for each other. I guess that we forgot our love and devotion to you both."

Ben stood up, and Cathy joined him. She was crying too much to speak. Her heart was breaking.

Their mother begged them to sit back down, and at the same time she was looking at their father with pleading eyes.

He seemed to come to a hasty decision, and nodded his head in silent agreement. Because he too, was too overcome to speak.

Their mother wiped the tears from her eyes, and gathered some of that inner strength that good mothers always seem to have. She sat erect, looking around at her family to get absolute attention.

Carina Marshall slowly and solemnly began the second part of the 'blessing in disguise' that Reverend Mother Segovia had spoken of. Now the blessing came, from the lips of a mother, to the ears and heart of a mother-to-be.

"Cathy, you and Ben are not flesh and blood. You're not brother and sister. As a matter of fact, you and he are not even remotely related, at least not by blood. The great sin which you have committed, is not so great after all.

"Cathy, I am your real mother. I bore you out of wedlock. The man who sired you, didn't want you *or* me. Your 'father,' sitting here at the table with us, *did* want you. And he wanted me. He married me. In truth, he is your father in the purest sense of the word."

Carina took a breath before continuing. "After we were married, it was discovered by my doctor that I couldn't give John the son that he so dearly wanted, so we... we... Ben, we adopted you! So your father would have a son, an heir to his name, and to the business he's worked so hard for. It's all for you, for you and Cathy when we are gone.

"It was our decision not to tell you that we are not your flesh and blood parents, Ben. John wanted our little family to be whole and full of love. And I tell you, we have covered you with love ever since we first brought you home. Even to this very moment in time.

"We are both Catholics in our hearts, and in our souls, but there is something in our marriage—in our being together—that the church would frown upon. Father O'Brien and Mother Segovia are aware of our shortcomings. They are also aware of who you and your sister truly are.

"We have come to the feet of God, the Virgin Mary, and of Jesus. We no longer feel that we have sinned against God.

"Even now, I can understand when Cathy says that she loves you, and when you say you love her. Cause in that way, I say to you, Ben, that I and your father are *not* sorry in any way that we failed to tell you that you were adopted.

"I only tell you now, because of the situation we find ourselves in. Otherwise, we would have taken the secret to our graves. Make no mistake about that fact."

She looked across the table. "Ben, you are our *son*. In the name of God Almighty, you are our own dear son!"

And Carina Marshall, could hold on no longer because her cup was running over. They hugged each other close, tasting the salt of each other's tears. Tasting the salt of the earth, and the blessings of God, the father of all things.

It was Cathy who began, "Credo in Unum Deum!"

The family joined her in reciting the creed. It was Ben who ended it, somewhat out of context with, "Gloria In Excelsis Deo!"

Ben hugged his father. Cathy hugged her mother. Then they switched places and hugged some more. There was no longer any need for mere words, because love took over and was in full command. Oh I tell you, it was such a wonderful time of pure love.

Tell me, do you think God agreed with them?

"Son, here's how we are going to do it," John said. "You and Cathy come on back home, and you can still complete college. Cathy, I'm sorry that you can't become a nun. But there are many other ways for you to help people.

"I'll ask Father O'Brien to announce in church that you, Ben, are really our adopted son. I'll even ask to post the adoption papers, so all can see them. You and Cathy cannot get married in the Catholic church, because you are already married in your hearts and that's where it counts... Before God.

"Let us remain the good family that we were, and shall always be, before God, and before our peers. We are going to stay together, to raise our grandchild in the same manner and with the same love that we raised our children with, our son and our daughter."

Ben graduated from college with high honors, came home and transformed his father's business into one of the largest, and most successful businesses in America.

The wrath of the people never once materialized. Yes, Father O'Brien made the announcement in church, and that was it. No one looked down on the Marshall family. If any looking was done, it was up, and certainly not down.

Cathy Marshall, bore her husband Ben, a fine boy, and they called him John O. Marshall. The 'O' was in honor of Father O'Brien.

Cathy worked tirelessly with the poor, the needy, and the homeless. In fact, she became a modern day missionary, right at home. A modern day angel of mercy, and everyone loved her so much.

The Marshall family lived long and well, in love, in good health, and in the bountiful mercy and blessings of God.

And they lived happily ever after.

## THE END

# INTRODUCTION

---

When I was a young lad, I was a loner. And because of that, I often spent a lot of time sitting on the front porch, observing all the people, the neighbors in our small community.

That was the way in which I became aware of a lot of closely guarded secrets. I guess the good folks became so used to seeing me around, that they no longer actually saw me. I became the Invisible Boy. I no longer existed to them, so they went about their little secrets with full vigor. And there was not too many of them that I didn't see.

If someone had asked me, I could have given a full accounting of the lives on the dark side, of most of the people that I saw every day. Fortunately, no one asked me. At least, no one asked me before I was wise enough to keep my mouth shut.

Sometimes I sat on the back porch, and sometimes I would be moving around, and seeing what I wasn't suppose to see. I knew who was doing what to who. You'd be surprised at what one lonely little boy can see.

No, I wasn't a peeping Tom. But there was absolutely no need to peep. I saw everything with my eyes wide open. Matter of fact, I would have to have been blind not to see the goings on. It was like watching a great big soap opera, and most of the people that I knew were the stars.

Oh I tell you, it was *Amos n Andy, Just Plain Bill, Steller Dallas, When a Girl Marries, Ma Perkins, Dick Tracy, Gang Busters,* and not to forget *John's Other Wife.* And all running at the same time. Plus, it didn't cost me a cent to watch. It was all free.

I guess a lot of folks thought that I was too young to know what was going down. But I fooled them, I knew exactly what house the postman would always go into and spend a long time. Which woman was playing the numbers on a daily basis, and if she hit, or not. Who stole the front tires for his car, and who he stole them from, I even knew *when* the deed was done.

I knew why the neighbor's dog suddenly up and died, why Mr. Williams walked wide legged, and who was putting grease on him. I knew who burned her neck bones 'n rice, and why. I knew why little Marie missed her period, and who was getting ready to catch the next thing smoking out of town.

That Bob Jenkins had all his cards marked, and it was J.J. who found out and blabbed. That's why Bob was lying out there in the hospital, wondering who had dropped a dime on him. Oh, and I also knew that the Reverend liked his whiskey straight, and his women big and mellow! Miss Minnie, the Rev's wife, liked her men skinny, just like Deacon Bradley.

I knew why Miss Lucy White, who played the piano in church every Sunday, wouldn't come out of her house for a whole week. She had a big mouse under her right eye, where her face had come into contact with the Reverend's fist.

And it went on and on!

You know, it was almost impossible to determine who was screwing who. Because it went on all day and half the night, least wise, until my mama made me go to bed.

It was like everyone was turned-on all the time. I saw folks jumping out of windows, hiding under the stairs, and running for all they were worth. I mean full out. It was like a sex maniac in a whore house with a gold credit card. Or the good folks were continually in heat. Oh if only they had those small movie cameras in those days, and I was smart enough to put it all on tape, I could have put *Candid Camera* and the *Funniest Home Movies* out of business.

Most of the women who stayed home all day had men friends, who came at a regular time, stayed with them all day, and left just before the husband arrived home after work. Oh, some of those husbands certainly were no angels. They had skates on their feet, just like their wives had. Talk about burning the candle at both ends.

Our next door neighbor had three different men sleeping with her, over and above her husband. I knew that some day she would have a mix up in schedules, and I was ready to watch the fight when it occurred. Man-ah-*man* did they have a wang dang doodle. Knocked out the windows, broke down the doors, and generally destroyed the place. All but one of the 'participants' spent some time in the hospital.

Most of the men, the runners, were always bragging about who they were sleeping with, and all of those doing the bragging had at least one woman on the line they were keeping a secret. But the *Shadow* knew who the secret lovers were… the *where*, and the *when*.

Let me tell you about one of the incidents that stuck in my memory, because it was so rare, and when one of the good husbands had *THE LAST LAUGH*…

# THE CAST:

1. **Valentino "Val" Boger**    The Husband

2. **Christine "Chris" Boger**    The Wife

3. **Perry Stafford**    The Boyfriend

4. **Mrs. Powell**    The nosy neighbor, who is always there

5. **Your Storyteller**    The seeing eyes that rarely miss anything

6. **The Rest...**    A wonderful supporting cast of everyday people

**Note:** It's a well-proven fact that it's impossible to do something without being seen, especially when you don't *want* to be seen. No matter how careful you *think* you've been, somebody will see you every time!

# THE LAST LAUGH

Val Boger worked in a steel mill. He had one of the hardest jobs in the plant. He held onto that job because the pay was very good, and he needed it to support his wife's lifestyle.

Oh, don't be sidetracked by his first name. You see, his mother was a movie lover, and one of her favorite stars was Valentino. So you guessed it... His first name was Valentino. But never mention that to him. Of course he preferred to be called Val, by friends and strangers alike.

In truth, Val is a pretty good guy, if you get to know him. You see, he's pretty much a loner, doesn't make friends easily.

But he was married. Once when he was in a rare talkative mood, he said that he'd been married a little over fourteen years. Said they had no children, and I could tell from his attitude and his tone of voice, that made him real sorry. I mean, not having kids.

He was a farmer, the salt of the earth, turned steel mill worker. Said that he was from a little place in Perkins County, not too far from North Platte, Nebraska. He once had his own farm, but had to sell it. Like I said, he was a real nice guy, if you could get close enough to know him.

He was a good hard worker, giving a full day's work in return for a day's pay. He'd been working at the mill for a little over three years when our story took place.

Old Jim McCormick was his foreman at the mill, and he was one of the first persons that Val invited into his home for dinner. Jim said it was a real nice place, in a good neighborhood. Val had used the money from the sale of his farm to pay for it.

I guess it was just like a lot of stories you hear. Val was a good hard working honest man, like I said, the real salt of the earth. He was an average American, in any way you took him. You know the kind; if you were a Soldier in a war and you needed someone to trust your very life to, then it would be Val. That was the kind of a man he was.

It's often said that behind every great man there is an even greater woman. But you know, the exact opposite of that old saying is sometimes true. 'Cause, you see, his wife was *not* the even greater woman.

Yes, she too was a farmer turned city dweller, but there was something very different about her. It was plain to see right away that she was different from her husband. Like night and day. Like black and white!

When he first invited me to meet Christine Boger (he called her Chris), I found her to be the kind of a woman that most men might call beautiful. When in reality, she was no more than pretty. What made her *seem* beautiful was the way she presented herself, the way she flaunted her body. She did it in such a way that she came across as a street walker, and her body seemed like the body of a whore. When I saw her, she was wearing an outfit that left nothing to be guessed at.

Mother Nature, or whoever is in charge of handing out such things, had given her some fine things to stare at. I looked at her body just like most men looked at her, and I saw what most men see in a woman.

When I first arrived, Chris made us a good J&B with coke, 'cause it was my favorite. Then Val showed me around his home, paying particular attention to his pride and joy, his workshop in the basement. Sure it made me envious, 'cause he had an outstanding workshop, with all the modern Craftsman tools and machines. Why, he had the very latest sander, plane and router combination, and a full-sized, band-saw that would cut through anything, from case hardened steel to paper and plastic. It was quite a set up.

The meal was also quite a set up, his wife Chris was a very good cook. The food was excellent, a very good example of American farm cooking.

I really did try not to, but I took the opportunity to really look at Chris. I was ashamed with myself, because I couldn't help but to find her physically attractive. Once again she was dressed for the occasion. She was something to look at, I had to give her that, with her fine long legs, beautiful round butt, and magnificent breasts. She had all the things that any man, living or dead, likes to see. Even a blind man.

As I said, her face was no more than pretty, but she had all the things that a man loves to see, and she was very well endowed with them.

I was very careful not to let Val see me checking her out. Once I had a good look, I didn't look again. But God forgive me, I couldn't help thinking, *if she was as good in bed, as her biscuits...*

You know something, the way she was dressed had me thinking things that no man should think about another man's wife. To my great sorrow, I couldn't stop thinking that way. When I looked into Val's eyes, I could tell that he knew exactly what was going on in my head.

Damn... That woman had no right to twist my mind that way. But she did!

Well, in spite of my short-comings, Val and me became good steadfast friends. We would often stop off at the corner tavern for a cool one, where he opened up about him and Chris.

It's quite normal for one man to talk to another man about the things that are bothering him. Maybe you do it because you're hoping someone else may have a better solution. Or maybe you just do it because sometimes you've got to talk these things out.

I really did feel sorry for Val. What it all came down to, it was Chris who had talked him into selling his farm, which had been in his family for over a hundred years. She wanted to move to the big city, and to make something of their lives past scratching in the dirt.

Truth was, Val was a dirt farmer born and raised. The lights of the big city could not and would not change that fact, or him.

But Chris thought she was too beautiful to waste her life on a damn farm. She was in love with her own body, and almost every man she met seemed to agree, so she must have felt justified in her belief.

Chris loved her own body even more than men loved it. She did special exercises, ate certain foods, took certain vitamins, and bought all kinds of contraptions to enlarge her breasts, firm her thighs, shape her already magnificent rear end, and to generally improve on a good thing.

She refused to have children, because being pregnant left stretch marks, and she had no intentions of marring her body. She also refused to adopt a child. She figured that was asking for somebody else's problems.

She spent big time bucks on her membership at an exclusive downtown Physical Boutique, where she often pumped iron. (Or was it that iron was pumping her?)

You know, it was during that conversation that I had the feeling that Chris was allowing her husband the pleasures of her body, only on very rare occasions. Val admitted as much, even that he suspected there was a younger man enjoying his wife's fine body.

And I had to agree. I felt sure that some man was riding her body like a Kawasaki motorcycle at the races. Of course I didn't tell him that, because the one thing that I was very certain of from my association with him, Val really and truly did love his wife. There wasn't one thing that he wouldn't do for her.

He had good reasons to believe that she was sleeping with another man. But he loved her so much that he was able to overlook those reasons, if it made her happy.

Chris wanted a new red Corvette, and he would get it for her, even though it would mean an additional bill and possibly a second job for him. Did you ever love someone that much?

In my mind, it was very difficult to come to terms with whether what Val was doing was right or wrong. Whether it was nobler to do things his way, or to blow the boyfriend away. To blow, or not to blow… that was the question.

During the next few months things became worse and worse in the Boger household. Chris changed boyfriends, and with the change she became bolder and bolder. And Val just seemed to grow a little smaller and smaller each time we stopped off for a few drinks.

I tried to get Val to have it out with his wife and her lover, but he would always stop me, saying that it was a personal matter of his, and it was up to him and him alone to figure out how to solve it. He had a point, so I clammed up.

Still, I couldn't help worrying about Val, because the last two times we went for a drink, he was very silent. He seemed to always be way off, in a world of his own. I had the feeling that world was his very own private hell.

Christine was spending more and more time in the Physical Boutique, and less and less time home with Val. And because of that, often when he came home from the mill, he had to fix his own meals and to generally take care of the housework as well. In fact, it was tearing him up inside and getting to the point that he was finding it very hard to turn the other cheek.

One late night when she came home, smelling of booze and cigarette smoke, he had to say something. 'Cause you see, up to that time, she neither smoked nor drank alcohol. When he confronted her, she didn't become angry like she did most of the times when he tried talking to her. Instead, she listened till he was run down, then she spoke in an almost apologetic voice.

Yes, she smelled of cigarette smoke because of the going away party she went to, and most of the people who were not pumping iron, were smokers. Yes, she had two drinks, because her new trainer said it was okay, even desired, that she consume a little alcohol every now and then. The alcohol was good for her stomach muscles and metabolism.

She apologized for the way things had been for the last few months, and promised to bring about a change. Why she even shed a few tears, promising a good supper the next day, and that she would be a better wife to Val. Starting that night, after a good hot shower, she wrapped her long sexy legs around him and sent his soul to the moon.

You bet, the next morning everything was A-Okay! Chris even told Val to take her car, the bright red Corvette, to work. Sure he was happy, 'cause she was even better in bed than her biscuits.

Want to know a secret? Okay, okay! But promise not to blab. Truth was, that night, Chris realized that she was caught. Busted. And just like she had always planned, she simply instituted Plan-A. Which simply was, to give Val a little—

which seemed like a whole lot to him—seeing as how it was so long since she last gave him *anything*.

Yeah, you guessed it. She used the age-old weapons from a woman's vast arsenal of weapons which are sure to get results. Sex and a full stomach, almost always guaranteed.

What man in his right mind can put up a workable defense against such old and proven weapons? If really good sex is compared to a nuclear explosion, the nuclear explosion comes out second best. No more than a paper cap.

Don't forget, Chris had big strong pretty legs, and her 'gold mine' was deep and tight from all those toning exercises. Plus, she had a lot of secret experiences in how to effectively use it. I guess she must have mushed Val's brains that night.

The following evening, she served him pot roast with all the trimmings, homemade apple pie, and a lot of other nice things from home. When she finished with that poor boy, he wasn't sure of his own name.

Talking about being used. Or was it misused? No matter, she made a clean getaway, and come out smelling like a rose. Clean as the board of health.

Things went well after those two nights. Well to tell the truth, things didn't change a whole lot. Val was just too spaced out to notice. Sometimes she would meet him at the kitchen door, wearing only her birthday suit. After that, he was blind as a bat. Couldn't see a damn thing.

Well, she took advantage of her husband for about another six months or so. But you see, her allowing him to sample her gold mine—her biscuits—had an undesired effect. Simply put, Val fell more and more in love with her, and because he honestly believed that her biscuits were truly the best in the world.

The thought of another man having her became unbearable. He was no longer willing to share. He wanted it all to himself. But that wasn't what *she* wanted.

At first she only did it to blind him, so that Val wouldn't notice that she was very much like the only car in a six-man car pool. Oh, the iron pumping her was beginning to show. It was starting to leave marks that were a lot worse than stretch marks ever dared to be.

That was the time when Val began to notice that things had not really changed at all. The only changes had been in his imagination.

When he confronted her that time, with the cigarette butts in the toilet and the cold suppers, she figured that her biscuits had erased enough of his mind for her to tell him to shove-it! And she did just that.

Sometimes I wonder… If Val had grabbed her right then, and whipped her till she was stark naked, maybe things wouldn't have gotten so far out of hand. Instead, he stomped off down to his workshop in the basement, and started making birdhouses.

He tried to let it go, like he had done so many times before. But he couldn't stop thinking about how good she was in bed, how good she made him feel when she shared that amazing whore's body with him. And he didn't want to lose the dream.

Someone—and Val had a very good idea of *who*—was taking his wonderful Chris away from him. And he vowed not to let that happen.

Sometimes, it takes a lot of pain and pressure for a man to turn. When a good man finally does turn under the weight of all that pain, he turns hard. And that's when things can get ugly. It's 'Katie bar the door!'

No, Val didn't beat up on his wife after all the wrong she did him. He was still too much a good man, a *real* man, to strike her. A good man doesn't beat his wife.

He thought of trying again to talk with her, to reason with her, but he remembered all those times before. Why he even figured out the 'bed and supper bit.' And while it surely was good, the best in the west, it wasn't *that* good! No… It was the time for a change.

But still he had to give it one last chance, so he went back upstairs and tried in vain to talk to her. Chris didn't come out and say that she was screwing around—not in so many words—but she *did* say that she had lost her love for him, that she wanted more than he could give her, and she wasn't talking about cars.

At one point, she became real angry and screamed that, "she might take everything away from him. That he would be lucky if, 'they' left him with a pair of dirty socks!"

Yes! Good man or not, he came close to punching her lights out. But he was smart enough to know if he did that, it would be just what 'they' wanted.

He was standing there looking at his wife, and really hurting, 'cause he knew for sure he was really *seeing* her for the very first time. And it was enough to make him physically sick. So he abruptly stopped auguring with her and went back down to the solitude of his workshop.

There *had* to be a better way.

Val went to work that day, clocked in, then went out across the rear lot and drove straight back home. He arrived in time to have a good position from which he could watch his house, where he could see who came and went—without him being seen by their nosy neighbor, Mrs. Powell.

He didn't have long to wait… It was a foreign-made car, a BMW, black and racy looking. The man who got out of the Beemer was sure of himself, and it was plain to see that this wasn't his first time at Val's house.

The man wore his hair in a long ponytail, and he was dressed to show off his Mr. America physique. He was well muscled, and the way he strolled boldly into another man's home, also meant that he was a bit short on brains.

Chris met the man at the door and brazenly threw her luscious self on him. They held onto each other and kissed for minutes.

Yes, Val was hurting! He moved to charge up to them and start swinging. To rush into his house, grab his Remington automatic shotgun, and blow both of them away.

He fought to control his anger, and focus his thoughts. What was the right thing to do?

He was looking around like a trapped animal when he noticed that there was another pair of eyes watching as his wife stood kissing another man. Mrs. Powell was on the job.

Val was quick to realize that—if Mrs. Powell was actively watching the scene between his wife and her boyfriend—there was a very good chance that nosy woman had been watching all along. She probably had it recorded in her mind, every time the boyfriend... or any other person... came and went.

Val forgot about Mrs. Powell. He had finally gotten a good look at the man's face. Even from the distance, he could remember where he had seen the man before, on one of the group photos from the Physical Boutique downtown. The man was one of Chris's "trainers."

Val was sure that the man wouldn't leave until shortly before Val was due to arrive home from work, so there was no sense in waiting for him now.

Careful not to be seen, Val returned to work. He hadn't been missed.

It was time for him to get down to some serious thinking and planning. No, he wouldn't be dumb enough to find himself in jail or prison. That would be giving his life's work into the hands of Chris and that mindless muscle.

He took off from work early enough to be watching for the black Beemer when it turned the corner onto the main street. He made sure it was the same license number. The car stopped at a favorite watering hole for the muscle-bound class. Yes, it was the ponytail, muscles and all.

Val waited. After about 40 minutes, Mr. Ponytail was on the way again, that time to his home to change, Val figured. And he was right again.

'Stafford, P.' was on the mailbox. Val was pretty sure that the 'P' didn't stand for 'Ponytail,' but he went on calling the man that anyway.

Once Ponytail was inside, Val pressed the buzzer beside the mailbox.

"Yeah?" the voice over the intercom sounded irritated.

Val asked for Mrs. Stafford.

"There is no Mrs. Stafford here," the voice snapped. "Only Mr. Stafford, and he ain't married. Now go the hell away!"

The intercom speaker went silent.

Val smiled. He was very careful to use the back entrance as he left. Ponytail answered his questions, nicely.

When Val got home, Chris gave him a Hungry Man TV dinner for supper. When he was throwing the aluminum tray away, he saw that there were two T-bone steak bones in the garbage, along with the aluminum wrapping from baked potatoes and salad.

Chris has served a fine meal—steak and all the trimmings—for herself and Mr. Ponytail. Val had gotten a TV dinner.

Now how about that? Val actually smiled, in anticipation of the coming events.

Chris made a half-hearted attempt at conversation, but Val didn't join in. In bed, she offered herself to him. He heard her audible sigh of relief when he refused her.

It took several minutes for it to hit her. This was the very first time Val had refused the offer of her body.

Val could almost hear her thinking. He was surprised, and rather proud of himself. Yes, he wanted her. But, to accept her would be the same as taking 'seconds' after Ponytail. No! Hell no!

Chris was shocked, but she decided that what she was offering, no man in his right mind could refuse twice. So she decided to wait. After all, her gold mine, her biscuits, were one of a kind. In a class of their own. Val would come crawling and begging her. Then, *she* would refuse *him*.

The next day, Val arranged his schedule to allow him to keep an eye on Mr. Ponytail. The man didn't get out of bed until around ten, showered, had coffee, then headed for the Physical Boutique.

Val watched the guy leave, and then waited just in case Ponytail forgot something. When he was sure that the man wasn't coming back immediately, Val entered the building and went straight to the man's apartment.

Getting in wasn't hard for a man as handy with tools as Val was. He was inside the place in less than the time than it would take to tell about it.

Finding out about Ponytail wasn't hard either. The man wasn't careful about keeping things locked up or out of sight.

Within a few minutes, Val knew that the man's name was Perry Stafford. He had been born in Pennsylvania, and he was more than twenty years younger than Chris.

It looked like Perry lived alone, but there was evidence of several female visitors. Val ignored these things, but he felt a stab of pain in his heart when he spotted panties, brassieres, and very private things belonging to his wife.

He also found exotic photos of Chris naked, and some with Perry deep inside her. Val chose some of her private things, and some of the private things belonging to Perry. He also took some of the explicit photos with him, just in case. Val had in his hands, proof positive that his wife had been screwing another man—the man with the ponytail, Perry Stafford.

He made a complete examination of Perry's apartment, and when he finally left back to work, Val had a very good idea about what kind of a man Perry Stafford was.

Val went to work, to start his shift. He knew what made Ponytail tick, now. He knew his distinct odor, and most of all... how to bring the man down.

When Val got home from work, he knew right away that Perry had left only minutes before. That was good. He put the things he had taken from Perry's apartment safely away, and waited.

Oh, he really made the day and night for his wife, when he refused her beautiful body for the second time. Now *that* upset her to no end.

If she was worried after his second refusal, she was nearly in a panic by the next night, when Val turned her down *again*!

Chris had to be nervous as hell. Something had gone wrong. She couldn't understand Val's reaction at all. It was impossible to even think of it... A man refusing to take her magnificent body? But her husband was doing the unthinkable for the <u>third</u> time!

Clearly, Val had lost his mind. (Or *found* it.) In any case, Chris was determined to make him suffer for turning his stupid back on her gold mine.

She began to wear less and less around the house, to wear those items of clothing that were a bit too small, too tight, and showing entirely too much of her luscious, sensually appealing body. You bet it was hard on Val. Don't forget he was her husband, and they were married longer than 14 years. He remembered the taste of her, the sweetness of her, and how indescribably wonderful it was to make love to her... to *have* her.

There were times when he saw her almost naked, that his stomach cramped so much that he wanted to throw up. He wanted cry like a little baby child. Misery was his constant companion. It was very hard to keep his feelings a secret from her. No man should have to suffer like Val suffered.

At the same time, Perry Stafford, was living off the fat of the lamb. He was going almost every day to a working man's house, eating that man's food, and screwing his wife.

A man like that doesn't deserve a quick death. That's what Val figured. A man who would do that deserves to suffer, like the woman's husband is suffering. And then the bastard should have his head blown off.

Val was a good Christian, his folks raised him that way. But he was very tired of turning the other cheek. And he was starting to think about how to kill his wife and her lover!

Time passed. Christine and Perry grew even more brazen in their affair. It appeared that she was deliberately trying to cause her husband as much pain and heartache as she could. And—I hasten to add—she was doing a very good job of it.

Of course by that time, their illicit relationship was well known by all of the neighbors. They had become the talk of the neighborhood. Mrs. Powell was one of the leading moderators, because she was just across the street from the action.

Val withdrew more and more into himself. Frankly, his work situation didn't help matters one bit. His job at the steel mill was to keep the feeding hoppers full of raw materials. From a central control room, he managed the automatic devices which loaded ore and scrap iron into the hoppers, which—in turn—fed the ladles and furnaces.

When he had come to the mill, it had taken eight men to do the job. Now, automation had reduced the eight man shift to a single man, sitting at a giant console. That one man was Val.

His area was at the back end of the mill adjoining the railroad yard. It wasn't very hard for him to come and go without being noticed. Because Val was a dependable worker, his supervisor, Jim McCormick, scarcely ever came out to check on him. It wasn't necessary.

Val kept his fridge loaded with beer and other goodies, and once in a while, Jim would drop by for a cold one. Other than Jim, most of the time Val was all alone.

If you ask me, I would say that Val's job made the whole situation even worse. He had too much time to think, and not enough people to talk to. So hour after hour, he thought about his beautiful wife and her lover.

They were no longer trying to hide what they were doing. It was an insult. It was *more* than an insult… It was an out an out assault on his manhood.

How would you would feel if your wife, the woman that you love, was doing the same thing to *you*? Not a very nice thought, is it? Think about what Val was dealing with…

Perry was a big strong he-man hunk of muscle. He was young, virile, and handsome. And from the odors left standing in the bedroom, he spent some time riding Chris like she was the lead horse in the Kentucky Derby.

And all that riding was beginning to tell on Christine. She was starting to show some wear-n-tear from too many rough rides with her much-younger lover. How 'bout *that*?

In truth the whole affair was killing Val. He tried real hard to live by the golden rule. You know, the one that says you should *love thy neighbor*? But look at what that golden rule was getting him… A constant kick in the butt.

This thought drove Val to reconsider all the stuff in the Bible, the Ten Commandments, and how good things were coming to him if he was peaceful and patient. But he didn't *want* to inherit the Earth. All he wanted was his wife.

Val came to the sad conclusion that the street version of the golden rule made one hell of a lot more sense. *"Love thy neighbor, but don't let her husband catch you."* That seemed a lot more realistic than the Biblical version.

*   *   *

Perry went on a two week visit to his parents. He drove Christine's Corvette for the trip, rubbing a little more salt in Val's wounds.

But Val decided to let that insult pass. While Perry was gone, Val was going to make a last ditch effort to talk some sense into the woman he still loved.

Now I don't know *how* it was that he still loved her, but he did.

Chris saw this as a golden opportunity to get back at Val for having the gall to turn down the offer of her body. She allowed him to kiss and fondle her, right up to the point of penetration. Then, she threw him off her, with full contempt.

Val almost lost it. He didn't quite raise a fist to her, but did slap her.

Chris promised if he raised his hand to her again, she would scream bloody murder, run out in the streets and yell her head off until the neighbors called the cops. If he laid a hand to her again, she would have him barred from his own house! And that wasn't all she said...

Her last words were the most hurting... "I won't miss you tickling me, with what you have. 'Cause I'll have a *real* big man to fill me all the way up with satisfaction!"

Now that really did piss Val off royally. He ran to the closet where his shotgun was kept. It was time to end it all, to blow her away. He was ready to go to jail for taking the only option Chris had left open to him.

It was her smiling face that brought him up short. Something was wrong. Chris knew where Val's shotgun, a 12-gauge Remington autoloader, was kept. But, she didn't seem afraid, knowing that he was angry enough to do her.

Common sense took control of Val's mind, heart, and body. He actually smiled back at her, and casually put his PJs back on. Then he went downstairs to sleep. He knew that if he stayed in the same room with his wife, he would surely kill her and suffer the consequences.

Val thought about Mrs. Powell. She *had* to know all about the affair between Chris and Perry. If something happened to Chris, would she tell her story to the court? Maybe. She would probably tell it all to the cops, the judge, and anyone else who would listen.

When the judge learned how Chris has been whoring around, would he consider that as a justification for killing her? Not a chance. Val wasn't an expert on the law, but he knew that his wife's affair would not help him. To the police and the courts, it would only count as Val's motive for murder.

Christine turned on him. She was like a female dog in heat, when it came to Perry. She had destroyed everything they had, for sex. Their marriage vows were completely dishonored. In her last hurtful remark, she had clearly admitted having sex with that mindless guided muscle. Perry Stafford—Mr. Ponytail—was no more than a super dildo, batteries included.

At his very first opportunity, Val checked his shotgun. Perry must have doctored it, 'cause the gun wouldn't fire. But Val had grown up around shotguns. It was an easy matter to make the necessary corrections. And he was ready to blow both their heads off.

Should he kill Chris first? Stick the barrel of the shotgun into the hole that she loved to have filled, and pull the trigger? Or wait to catch them both in the act, and do both of them, one at a time? Let his unfaithful wife watch him emasculate Mr. Ponytail, using a 12-gauge scalpel?

Val didn't give the slightest consideration to taking his own life. If he shot Chris, the state would take care of that for him.

He was going into the bedroom to do her when common sense hit him, and he paused. Why be stupid about it? Why not kill two birds with one stone, as the old saying goes?

So Val decided to wait until Perry returned from visiting his family. By that time, Chris would be as hot as a two-dollar special on Saturday night. And Perry would be eager to drive her up the wall, just as hard as he drove her new Corvette.

So Val waited, and watched. He was like an old vulture waiting for the right time, then he would spring upon them and pluck their eyes out. What goes around was fixin' to come around. Amen!

When he got back into town Perry called Chris, and said that he was sorry, but he had a fender bender with her car. She said that was okay; Val would take care of getting it fixed. All she wanted Perry to do was hurry over and put out the fire between her legs, 'cause that fire was threatening to consume her.

Perry promised to send her soul to the moon and back. They set the date and the time.

Val was listening in, and promised himself that he would be in on that festive occasion.

To tell the truth, he wasn't sure what to do. You might think it's easy to kill your wife, especially if she's unfaithful. But it's not like in the movies, or those long running TV soap operas. The actors die, and then get back up to play their parts again. But if you stick the business end of a 12-gauge shotgun between a woman's legs and pull the trigger, she is *not* getting back up. Plus there is always the cold hard fact that the law frowns on that kind of thing.

To make matters worse for Val, he still loved Chris. Plain and simple as all that. I can't figure that out. Can you?

After all that was said and done—after the explicit photos, and the all evidence, and his own wife's admission—Val still was hoping that it was a bad dream. He kept hoping that he would wake up in her arms and holding her close, like old times. He had to see it for himself. He had to *see* Perry in bed with Chris, before he could truly believe it.

Val arranged to take off from work on the day of Perry's return. Of course, Chris didn't know about it. Val got up, ate his breakfast, and left in the morning, just like he was going to the steel mill.

As she planned her first day with Perry in two whole weeks. Chris laid in t-bone steaks, shrimp cocktail, fine California wines, and all the trimmings. There were two candles placed at the head of the bed, and a mirror positioned where Perry could see himself making love to her. He really did, care more for how he looked, than how she looked. He liked to see himself *working*.

Val didn't drive to the steel mill that morning. He parked his car in the lot at the mall, and walked back to his house. He entered through the back door, but Chris was far too busy getting ready to notice her husband returning home. Val simply sneaked down to the basement, and waited.

The stage was set.

Perry arrived around nine thirty, and Chris was all over him like white on rice. The only part of him she didn't kiss was the bottom of his feet, and that was 'cause he had his sneakers on.

"Doll, I'm hungry," Perry said. "Let's eat first. Then we can…"

But Christine was far beyond being hungry, for food, that is. She half drug him into the bedroom, ripping off both his clothing and hers as she hurried toward the bed.

Val was already up from the basement, and watching the heartrending scenes. He couldn't believe his eyes. Never, in their 14 years of marriage, had Chris ever acted that way over *him*.

At one point—as Val was sneaking up the stairs—he tripped and fell. His eyes were so full of tears that he couldn't see.

But Chris and her lover were too far gone to hear a full 21 gun salute.

By that time, Perry was caught up in the moment. The candles were already lit, and casting a soft glow across the darkened room.

Val crawled along the wall and entered Chris's clothes closet, from which he had a ring-side viewing position.

Chris was making sounds like a person gone stone crazy. By that time they were both in their birthday suits. Naked as jay birds in January. She was making little gasping sounds, admiring the huge tool of her very own self-starting mindless muscle.

Suddenly, Val had enough. He wanted out, he didn't want to see any more, for fear of losing his mind completely.

He remembered his dear mother repeating that old saying about, eavesdropping. Sweet Jesus, that old saying was true. He would leave the closet, but before he could sneak out, Perry bumped into the door, and it swung nearly closed. For him to get out, Val would have to move the door, which might give him away.

He had never in his life been so hurt, so saddened, that his heart was actually aching. And he was so dizzy it was hard to keep his balance.

Val almost burst into insane laughter, thinking that he was so stupid, he had gone into *her* closet, instead of *his*, where the shotgun was waiting.

He couldn't hold back the insane giggle, when realized that he had forgotten to reload the gun. The damn thing was empty. If he wanted to shoot someone, he'd have to find the shells. And right now, he was so confused, that he couldn't remember where he had put them.

He was over 40 years old, and Perry was bigger and stronger. If he went after the younger man, he would probably get his butt whipped. Again, he couldn't hold back a giggle at the thought. Even he could tell that he was very close to losing it. I mean going all the way around the big bend in the road.

They were on the bed, Perry was looking into the mirror, as Chris made the woman from that movie 'Deep Throat' look like a baby sucking the nipple of a bottle of milk. 'Cause Chris was doing the whole damn bottle.

At one point, Val thought she was going to make all of the six-foot plus young man, just disappear into her seemingly bottomless mouth.

Val was very close to fainting, cause it took her damn near five minutes to completely disgorge Perry's tool from her throat.

Val's knees gave way, and he almost fell, making one hell of a racket. But Perry and Chris were too far gone to care.

Perry mounted Chris like a stud bull, and she screamed.

Actually, both she and Val screamed at the same time, so it was impossible for Perry to distinguish between the scream from the closet and the one from her mouth. On the other hand, was there a difference?

Val turned his head, he couldn't look. He couldn't see anyhow, through the tears and the red haze of onrushing insanity.

Perry was stroking for all he was worth. Chris was screaming and begging for even more. Begging for her young lover to screw her even harder.

Finally, Val couldn't take it any longer! "Stop!... Oh my God! Please! Stop! Don't *do* that to her! She's my wife. I... I... I... I *love* her! Stop it, you bastard!"

He was pitifully screaming, and begging. Not real loud, sort of like he didn't want the neighbors to hear him.

He burst out of the closet and came to stand close enough to see the sweat on their convulsing bodies, to feel the heat of their passion, to smell the musky odor of their torrid love making. For reasons that escaped even him, he didn't attack Perry, or attempt to throw him off her. And that was very strange, considering the fact that he wanted Perry off Chris with all his heart and soul.

Chris was too far gone for it to matter, her eyes were so clouded with ecstasy that she couldn't see him. I don't think she even heard her husband begging her super stud to stop pounding her. She was enjoying it far too much to give a damn. On cloud 9, 10, and 11.

Instead of trying to kill them—which would have been perfectly normal, all things considered—Val was crying like a baby! Can you understand that?

He was shaking his head in disbelief. Trying to make it all go away. His mouth was filled with bile from his stomach and liver, mixed with the blood from his clenching teeth and gums. He was real close to puking his guts out.

Both Perry and Chris were caught by total surprise. Perry didn't jump off her. He just stopped pumping, staring in wide-eyed disbelief, his tool still imbedded deeply inside Chris.

"Don't stop!" Chris pleaded. "Give it to me! I need it *now!*"

She was begging Perry, in the same urgent and painful tone that Val was using. It was pitiful. She really was too wrapped up in the moment to care, too close to falling off the mountain. She was blind, even though her eyes were wide open. Unhearing, 'cause of the bells ringing in her ears.

You see, through it all, her magnificent body didn't stop its motions. It was still gyrating and urging Perry on, as her hands were clutching him, and her big strong legs held him in a steel vice-like grip. At the same time she was pulling him as deep as possible down into her bottomless pit.

Oh it was a scene like never witnessed before. Chris was acting like her husband wasn't standing there, watching her lover screw her.

Val had gone to all that trouble to get the final hard proof of his wife's unfaithfulness. When he *had* that proof, he had no idea what to do with it. His original plan of killing her was lost in the truth of what he saw. Yes, he had the proof, but, didn't know what to do with it.

Instead of coming out the closet like a roaring lion, ripping and tearing, he was crying and begging like a pussy cat.

Oh it grieves me to no end to tell you what happened. You should have seen him, standing there, bawling like a little baby boy, twisting and wringing his hands, instead of Perry's neck.

His eyes were glazed over, and badly out of focus. Had the whole affair been too much for him to bear? Had his mind snapped under the tremendous pressure?

I think you will readily agree that no man should have to bear witness to what Val saw, and heard, and felt.

Did he still love Chris? You bet he did. 'Cause you see, if you truly love someone, it's impossible to turn it off. That's one of the very sad things that our Maker built into each of us. Careful that it don't happen to you. Sometimes secrets have a way of becoming known.

Was it too much for one man to bear? Was it too much for one mind, for one heart to bear? There are recorded instances of smaller strains, that completely fried a man's mind.

Yes! He still loved her. Even as she cried out to the other man, still deeply inside her.

"Perry baby, don't stop. Now! It doesn't matter that he knows. I love you, I need you *now*! Give it to me, Baby. *Please*!"

Believe it or not, Perry began to respond to her cries, to what her body was doing to his body. He hadn't lost his urge. Remember, he was a man who liked to have a mirror positioned so he could watch himself work. A chauvinist. And there he was with an audience, a public of one, perhaps it was an opportunity that he couldn't let pass.

Anyway, he began to answer her begging and pleading, he began anew thrusting into her. As she urged him on to new heights. Oh it was one weird scene to him, it was the very first time he had taken a woman with her husband standing there, watching. And Perry just *had* to perform. He had to show the crying fool just how much of a man Perry Stafford was. Can you believe it?

Perry was like a man possessed. I think he lost a little of whatever mind he may have had running around in all of his bulging muscles. Every time he thrust into Chris, she screamed in ecstasy.

Val was screaming also, but not in ecstasy. He was screaming in pain, and I mean pain in its purest state.

"No! No!" He yelled. And that time, he actually tried to pull Perry off of Chris, and she called him a string of names too foul to print. At the same time, Perry swatted Val away like a pesky fly.

Val was propelled backward, reeling and crashing into the closet. But this time, it was *his* closet. And his hands were suddenly full of his very own Remington. He actually started giggling like the mad man he had become.

Chris was screaming with pleasure, and Perry was grunting with each powerful thrust. Their bodies slapping together in the age old rhythm of pure sex. Even Perry didn't know what was driving him like the mindless muscle that he truly was. He *had* to do it, 'cause he didn't know anything else to do. It was all that he had.

Val heard the sickening sounds of their bodies slapping together, of their loud animal grunting. Of his wife chanting over and over again, "Yes! Yes! Yes!"

Perhaps, it was Chris begging her lover to continue... Perhaps, Val flipped out all the way... Perhaps, it was the pleasure and contempt that shone in Perry's eyes... Perhaps, Val was suddenly, unexplainably sane... As sane as the Pope.

He stepped close to the bed and stuck the shotgun in Perry's sweating face.

Perry's eyes grew real big, and this time, he dismounted. Very forcefully disengaging himself from Chris, and she was crying like a feeding baby when the nipple comes out its mouth.

For the first time, Perry showed a little sense and froze in place. Even Chris stopped begging, and her eyes were suddenly clear. She looked at the shotgun, and smiled.

That's when Val knew that it was Chris, not Perry, who has doctored his gun. Perry didn't have the brains to do it. He was all dick, and nothing else.

Val answered his wife's smile with a cold hard grin of his own. "I know what you're thinking, Chris. But you're wrong. I found what you did to the firing mechanism, and I fixed it."

And suddenly, both Chris and Perry's butt holes were so tight that they ceased to exist. Perry rolled all the way off her.

"Don't you move again, you stupid bastard," Val snapped. "I'm going to give both you and your bitch time enough to kiss your ass good bye."

He jacked the slide of the shotgun, with a heavy metallic thump.

Perry almost fainted. His once mighty tool was as limp as a wet noodle, almost disappearing into his body. And then the urine began flowing. Perry was peeing on himself.

"Hold on man," the muscle-boy whimpered. "Please don't kill me. Please! It's all *her* fault, not *mine*."

Perry pointed a shaking finger toward Chris. "She came after me, mister. Understand? Yeah, I finally said okay, after she started paying my rent, and, giving me money. But I didn't go after *her*. Look at her... She's almost as old as my Mama!"

Val looked at his wife, lying naked on the bed, deserted by her young stud.

"I'm just a kid," Perry said. "Maybe I did you wrong, but not like *she* did. Man, if you kill me, you're going to jail for life, or to the chair. Am I worth that? Because she sure as hell isn't!"

You know, for a mindless hunk of muscle, that boy was suddenly, making a lot of good hard sense. Maybe he was doing a bit of growing up, even if it was on the wrong end of a shotgun.

"Please," Perry pleaded. "If you let me go, you'll never see me again. I'm real sorry! I lost my head, 'cause frankly, she ain't that good. And I sure as hell don't love her. Oh man... I'm *real* sorry."

Chris made a painful sound as her lover's cutting words sunk home. But she knew that what he said was true. This wasn't love. It was lust. She was in it because Perry was so damn good in bed. She would run rabbits, eat cow dung, and bark at the moon, rather than to lose his *services*.

Perry's little speech had a sobering effect on Val. The young idiot had a point about one thing. If Val blew them away, he would rot in prison, or worse.

All of a sudden, all Val wanted was to go back home to Nebraska. He would find him a nice farm, and go back to doing what he did best. Without Chris.

Val couldn't pull the trigger, he couldn't shoot them, not even if he had still wanted to. He had racked the slide of the Remington on an empty chamber. The gun still wasn't loaded, and he *still* didn't know where his shotgun shells were. But Chris and Perry didn't know that.

He jabbed the barrel of the shotgun in Perry's direction. "Put your clothes on, and get out of my sight, out of my house. Move! Before I change my mind and blow your stupid ass all over the place."

Val nodded toward Chris. "Oh, and take this piece of shit with you."

"Yes, sir!" Perry said, even as he was grabbing his clothes and quickly putting them on. He paused, smiling apologetically and not wanting to piss Val off, or press his luck, when he added. "But I don't want her, sir. Really…"

Val shook his head. "The only reason I don't pull the trigger right now, is that I don't think either of you are worth it. Suddenly I feel good, and I don't want this sick bitch either. She's all yours. Now, either you take her with you, or you're both cold meat!"

Chris was staring at her lover. "Perry, I told you two months ago that I'm pregnant," she said. "And you know damn well it's *yours*. I'm carrying your baby, and you talking about you don't want me? I'll see both of you in hell first."

Perry buckled his belt with a jerk. "Yeah, you told me that bullshit, Chris. But I know it's a lie. You're too damned old to have no baby. So why don't you just shut your lying mouth, and beg your husband to forgive you? 'Cause he's a better man than I'll ever be. Besides, he still loves you. If it was me, I would've blown you away a long time ago."

"Oh you sniveling bastard," Chris sneered. "After all the money I've given you… After all the times you've banged me, and said I was the best… Now cause he has a gun on you, you crawl like a snake to save your ass. Oh you… you… you…"

"That's enough, Christine!" Val growled. "Put your clothes on and get the hell out of my house now! Before I lose control and drop your laundry, even if I have to go to jail. It might be well worth it, to see you dead."

"You're no better than a common five-dollar whore," he said. "And the sight of you makes me sick to my stomach."

There was something about the way he said it, the sudden light in his eyes. She knew Val well enough to know that he meant everything he said. That it was best for her to shut up, and do what he said.

She put her clothes on, and took only her purse, thinking that it was a good sign that Val hadn't told her to pack anything. He would be begging her to come back in a day or two.

So she and Perry walked out to her Corvette. She could see some of the neighbors watching them as they drove away.

She was yelling at Perry as they turned onto the main street, shouting that he had let her down.

Perry was silent, thankful to God and to Val, for his life.

Val put the empty shotgun back in the closet, and took the soiled bedding down to the laundry room. At that time he was as sober as a federal judge, and absolutely feeling no pain. Fact was, he hadn't felt so damn good in a very long time. Sure, he felt ashamed of himself for crying, and begging Perry to stop screwing Chris.

He admitted to himself that she really didn't love him, and hadn't for years. All that time he had been fooling himself, and he knew it. Yes, he still loved her. But he had learned in that short space of time, watching another man screw his wife, to control his love for her. He would never again tell Chris that he loved her. It would be his secret.

He put the bedding into the washing machine, and wondered how much the neighbors had heard from his encounter with Chris and her lover. It was the time of day when most folks were not home, even in his neighborhood, most of the wives were working. There were a few of them at home taking care of their small kids, but not many.

Val was reasonably sure that no one had seen him come home, just as he was reasonably sure that someone had seen Chris and her super stud leaving. But that was okay. He would be rid of her, and no one would be physically hurt.

He would sue her for a divorce. Perhaps, he would be able to get Mrs. Powell to tell what she knew, and he wouldn't have to pay Chris alimony. It was a comforting thought.

He was shaking a bit, so he went to the fridge for a cold beer, and saw all the fine food that Chris had laid in for her and

Perry. He sat at the kitchen table, thinking. Maybe he should fix one of the T-bones for himself.

Then he thought about the neighbors, and he hoped that no one except Chris and Perry knew that he was home. No, it was better if he left right away, went for his car and returned as normal. At that point it really didn't matter, but somehow, he figured Mrs. Powell would be more on his side if she thought that everything happened without his knowledge.

So he would go get his car, then come back and enjoy the T-bone. In truth, food was far from his mind.

The beer wasn't even half gone when he heard Chris behind him.

"You can't just throw me out after all these years," she said. "No matter what I did, I'm still your legal wife."

Val was stunned. He hadn't heard her come into the kitchen.

"This is my house too," Chris said. "I have my rights, and you know the law will be on my side. So you and I best talk things out. I know what I did was wrong, but what's done is done."

Chris stood before him, just like nothing ever happened. She was even smiling.

Val remained silent, his mind running a mile a minute, trying not to succumb to her powers over his heart.

"If it will make you feel any better about not hurting Perry, he was right... It was me all along. Val, what you did today was to make him no longer want me. He put me out of my own car, near the alley. Then, he took off. So I came up the alley and in the back way. Didn't want my nosy neighbors to see me coming back to my own house."

Val was still silent, thinking.

Chris decided to press on with her demands. When she spoke again, it sounded like an order. "You and me got to talk, and we got to talk *now*."

It was still fresh in Val's mind, Chris telling her lover that she had to have him *now*!

And he also heard her telling her young lover that she was pregnant, carrying his baby. Yet, in all the years she had been married to Val, she had flatly refused to bear him children—for fear of stretch-marks.

Without another word, she started upstairs to the bedroom and Val was right behind her. So far, it was going just like she had planned.

"Okay," she said. "So I was wrong, and you caught me doing something that I'm sorry for. Let's just forget it. Forget that it ever happened, and things will get back to the old way.

"I know that you still love me. You loved me before you caught me, and you still love and want me. You want me *now*... You *saw* what kind of a woman I can be, and you want me now more than you ever wanted me before."

Val said nothing. Chris must not have noticed the look on his face.

"You agree to forget what happened," she said, "and I'll give it to you right now. And I promise that you will remember it forever..."

She gave Val a sexy look. "Come on, my husband. Take me, like Perry was doing when you caught us. I'm still on fire!"

Poor Val, he had to stand as far away from her as the room would permit. Yes! He wanted her. She was right, just like always. He still loved her with all his heart. But he would not say so.

Chris began to softly whisper the words, "Love the one you're with..." At the same time, she was twisting and gyrating her fine body, and stripping off her clothes as she danced. Piece by piece.

It was maddening to Val. He wanted to run away, but his legs refused to move to cooperate.

Oh I tell you, her belly dancing was enough to raise the dead.

She danced close to him and he could smell her musky odor, as she dropped her brassiere at his feet, and swung her magnificent large breasts in his face.

About half way between where Val was standing and the bed, she dropped her last piece of clothing to the floor. It was a golden colored pair of string panties. The kind with very little front, and only a string in the back.

She stood by the bed, waiting totally naked, fondling herself between her legs and her breasts. You're damn right, she was literally driving him *mad*!

"Come to me," she whispered. "Come on, take me. Take what is yours. Take what you would rather die than to lose. Come on, my husband... Do the right thing... Take your first step to Paradise."

Val suddenly found his voice. "Wrong! If I took that first step towards you, I wouldn't be crazy with desire. I would be just plain old crazy! After what you did to me, it's all over. I don't want you anymore. I don't love you anymore. Just get the hell out of my life."

He glanced around the room. "You want this place? You can *have* it. I'm going back home."

His eyes turned back to his cheating wife. "Let's face it, Chris... You are *not* the girl I married. And you sure as hell are not the woman that I want any longer. What I want is for you to pack your things and get the hell out. Or, I'll pack my things and get the hell out! I honestly don't care which."

He gave her a thin little smile. "Baby it's *over*. The fat lady just finished singing!"

It was time for Chris to lose it. She stood there, not believing what he had just said. Her mouth was working and forming words, but no sound came forth. That's when she curled her fingers into claws. She charged at him, her face twisted in pure rage and hate.

Half-way to him, her feet became tangled in her golden string panties. She tripped and fell forward, twisting slightly to her right, trying to break her headlong fall. It didn't work. Her head struck the corner of her beauty table with a sickening crunch. She crashed to the bedroom floor, and didn't move again.

Christine died instantly. A victim of herself.

Or, could it have been "someone" correcting an error, a mistake. Could it have been, the old saying, "What goes around, comes around?" And the coming around was at hand?

In any case, Val was no stranger to the cold faces of death. He knew that dull popping sound was her neck breaking. She was dead. However, being the good man that he was, he had to check it out—to physically look for any sparks of life. And there was absolutely no spark! Chris was in the hands of the Grim Reaper.

It had all happened so quickly, so quietly, so suddenly. Val was stunned with the suddenness of his wife's '*Final Act.*' He rushed to the phone to call for help. 'Cause it was the natural thing to do.

He was dialing 9-1-..., when the realization hit him full force. "Help for *what*? She's grave-yard dead. She doesn't need a doctor. An undertaker would be more appropriate. Besides, let's face it… Everyone will say that *I* killed her." He set the phone down.

It was definitely time to do some real serious thinking. His very life depended on what he did next. The neighbors had clearly seen Chris and Perry leave the house, and there was a good chance that Chris had been seen returning. There was a slight chance that Val hadn't been spotted coming into the rear of the house, but of course, anything you do, *someone* will see you. It was a cold hard fact.

Val had taken off from his job, which would be seen as premeditation. Perry would attest to the fact that Val had been in the house. A jury would determine that he had *planned* to kill his wife. He had caught them in bed—in the act, so he clearly had a motive to kill her. He had even threatened to kill them with a shotgun, another fact that Perry would attest to.

Chris was laying on the bedroom floor completely naked, and completely dead. She was a victim of the classic 'blunt instrument' of death.

Val was the only person in the house with her, and—to the entire world—*he* would be the person who struck her with a blunt instrument and killed her. Or the person who threw her down, slamming her head into the beauty table, killing her.

No matter how you said it, he would be the man who murdered his wife in a fit of anger, after catching her in bed with her lover. Period!

The testimony of Perry and the neighbors would be Val's ticket to the gas chamber, the electric chair, or that lethal injection they sometimes used for executions. No matter how you looked at it, he was doomed.

Doomed to die for something he hadn't done. His wife's death really had been an accident, but who would believe him? If he could afford a *dream team* of lawyers, even better than the Juice trial, *they* might be able to get him off with only a hundred years.

"Valentino my friend, you are up shit's creek without a paddle. Even if you could afford the best team of lawyers in the world, they couldn't save your ass. Matter of fact, if I was on the jury and heard all the evidence piled up against me, *I* would vote myself guilty too."

He had to sit down, and run it all by himself one more time, as he stared dry eyed at the still-desirable form of his dead wife. Her body was truly magnificent, even in the arms of death, and rapidly cooling down for the last time.

He felt truly sorry for her. Yes, he had thought of killing her, but when it came right down to it, he hadn't been able to do it. But she was dead anyway. He would have to tell her family, to tell his family. And even *they* wouldn't believe him. It would be hard for his own mother to believe.

"She stopped loving you long ago," Val said to himself. "If she ever loved you at all. Is it worth your dying for, or going to prison for the rest of your life? Think about it, is there a way out? And if there is, you have nothing to lose by trying it."

He covered her big beautiful body, so he wouldn't have to see her that way, and then he could think clearly! He looked at his watch. It was still morning; the day was still young. Everything had happened in a short period of time, those circumstances which changed his life forever. It was left up to him to pick up the pieces... try to salvage whatever he could, and that probably wasn't very much.

It only took him a few minutes to think up a plan. He didn't know if it would work, but he had to try *something*. Tell me, what would *you* do, if you were in his place?

Val checked outside, and all seemed normal. He steeled himself with cool rationality, and—thinking with his mind, not with his heart—he began scheming to survive.

Sometimes, talking or doing things with your heart can cause a lot of pain, and get you into more trouble than you can imagine. Take Val for instance... You know, maybe it was his heart that got him into the mess he was in. Being in love is not always a beautiful garden of roses. Sometimes, there's so much pain tagging along with love, that it's not worth it. At times like those, it's a hell of a lot less painful *not* to be in love. Think about it.

Val looked around the bedroom. There was no blood. No broken furniture. No alarm had been given. All was peaceful and quiet.

He picked Chris up and carried her to the basement. Their large chest-style deep freezer had been purchased to hold the eatable parts of a large buck, when deer season was in. For now, it would hold Chris nicely, until Val had time to...

Once Chris was safely and lovingly tucked-in, Val went about gathering the things she had worn, and putting them into a trash bag, all except her handbag.

When that was done, he very carefully went over everything again, checked the time, and began the second stage of his plan.

He put a pair of coveralls on over his clothes, with a color that closely matched the kind that city-workers often wore. Then he crawled on his hands and knees to the garage, keeping well below the level of the windows.

When he reached the garage, he chose a clipboard with a few sheets of paper attached, slipped out the side door to the alley, and casually walked away. He pretended to be busily making notes as he went, just like a city worker going about his business.

Once he had his car from the mall parking lot, Val shucked off the coveralls and drove directly to the ball park, to take in a game. He bought a ticket, and making sure to speak personally to the ticket seller and the ticket taker so they would remember seeing him.

Val and old Charlie Perkins were good friends. Charlie sold hot dogs, and had the memory of an elephant. He remembered all his good customers by their first names, and Val was definitely a good customer.

After the game was over, Val drove to Perry's house. The Corvette belonging to his wife wasn't there, but he didn't panic.

He drove to the Physical Boutique, and there was the car. It was easy for Val to put Christine's handbag under the front seat, where he hoped that Perry would find it.

Then he drove home, just like nothing happened.

He even waved a friendly greeting to Mrs. Powell, which wasn't out of the ordinary. He often did that whenever he saw her. Oh, he definitely caught the look of pity on her face, for a good man who wasn't aware that his loving wife was a slut.

Val smiled back, hoping that he was the only one with the secret... His slut-of-a-wife was *dead*.

Once inside the house, he made sure that all was as he left it. Then he drove to the store for some beer, so that when he returned he could park his car in the garage, where Chris normally parked the 'Vette.

When he went to the basement, everything was again normal. He had a large piece of strong plastic from work, which he very carefully spread on the floor. He laid her body just as carefully on top of the plastic sheet.

Now there is where it got real sticky. 'Cause no matter how much Val told himself that he was saving his life, it didn't work. He had to throw up three times, and was close to fainting the whole time that he was sawing her body into parts small enough to manage. Those parts were carefully placed into plastic bags.

There was no blood problem. Putting her body in the freezer, and cutting it up before it was too hard frozen solved the blood problem nicely, and the plastic caught all of the other residue.

You know, it didn't take him long at all. Not for a man who dressed-out and butchered deer almost every year. The hardest part was coming to terms with butchering his wife. Once he got over *that*, it wasn't much different from dressing out a six point buck.

In case you are wondering how he overcame his revulsion to butchering his dead wife, well it was like this... He simply thought of her begging another man to screw her harder, while Val had stood their crying and begging her to stop.

While removing her head, he had to grin, whispering to her, "Sweetheart, I guess today was the last time you will ever deep throat a man. Unless that old song is true, and *there's a gold mine in the sky*."

It really didn't take long; the torso was the most difficult. When it was dark enough, Val carried the plastic bags full of his wife out to the car, and put them all into the trunk, along with the plastic, the hand saw, and everything he had used to butcher her.

I'll bet you thought he would use that state-of-the-art Craftsman band saw to cut her up. But do remember, Val was a farmer, a hard working man, and husband. Oh he was a lot of things, but *fool* wasn't one of them.

As soon as the car was packed, he once again checked everything, making sure he hadn't overlooked any signs of what he had done in the basement.

Finally, he drove down to the mall, went in for a couple hooks of J&B with coke, shot the breeze with Mack the bartender, and drove back home. He parked his car in front of the house, as usual. Remember, Chris always parked the 'Vette in the garage. Only that night she couldn't, 'cause she was in the trunk of his car, all in pieces.

Val gave it a shot to fix one of the T-bones, but somehow that wasn't the thing to do. Once he could leave the toilet, he concentrated on the latter part of his farewell to Christine.

The next morning, he arrived early to work, just like always. Maybe even a few minutes earlier than usual, but most people probably wouldn't notice. His wife's torso went into the hopper with the larger pieces of scrap iron. Then the smaller bags and pieces went in with the ore and basic materials.

He used only three hoppers, the ones feeding the furnaces that required the most extreme temperatures. The drain off and the removal of the cooking slag was handled automatically. If there was any evidence left over from his wife after the *cook*, it would be totally unidentifiable. Those furnaces ran at a temperature far exceeding the furnaces used in human body cremations. The bag containing the sheet of plastic, the saw, and every item used in the basement went into the melting pots.

In less than 20 minutes he was finished. He moved his car to his normal parking place, and started checking his records and having his first cup of coffee. No one had noticed a thing.

His foreman, Jim McCormick, stopped in for a cup of coffee and a friendly chat, but that wasn't a problem. Jim did that sometimes, so the unexpected visit didn't worry Val. It might even be helpful, since Jim could now attest that Val had been doing his job, just like usual this morning.

They talked for a while about the job. It turned out that Jim wanted to promote Val to a foreman's position. Also, he felt real bad about not being able to help Val with his personal problems. Old Jim tried very hard not to say it, but it was clear to Val that his foreman was a good friend. It was also clear that his foreman knew about Chris and her boyfriends.

From the brief conversation regarding his problems at home, Val figured it out that most of the guys working with him knew about his wife's whoring ways. His family problems were definitely not a secret, but Val could live with that. Time was on his side.

Ain't it funny how a woman can take all the men in her neighborhood to bed, and everybody know about it except her husband? And believe it or not, if the cheating wife decides to dump her husband, she could still take everything from him— even the shorts off his butt—complete with skid marks. The law will still make the poor husband pay... Actually take his hard earned money to support that woman and her boyfriends.

Think about it.

I guess when thinking about that fact, it made it a hell of a lot easier on the poor husband, Val Boger, as he went about insuring that all his plastic sacks were consumed by the furnaces. The steel mill he worked for had the best electric crucibles in the city. The processing systems in making first rate steel would automatically purge the molten metal of all impurities.

By ten fifteen that morning, Mrs. Christine Boger had been vaporized in the pouring of three crucibles of fine steel. Val figured that was a fitting end for a woman who lusted for hard things.

In that way, Chris became a part of the steel girders going into a new skyscraper, part of some high pressure valves in an oil field, a few automobile frames, and some railroad tracks. Val even crawled into the hopper chutes, and checked the 'throw-off bins,' to make positively sure that no trace of his cheating wife was left.

Finally he returned to his giant control console with the satisfaction that none of her physical body parts would come back to haunt him. He would never again have to stand by his bed and watch a man screwing her. Never again have to listen to her begging that man to, "give it to me harder!"

That was when he broke down and cried. Perhaps you don't think that he was a good man, perhaps even he had his very own doubts about himself. Because he would have to look at himself in the mirror for the rest of his life. Yes, that would be his punishment, no doubt about that fact.

He ran outside, into the vast noisy railroad yard, and he screamed until his voice faded away. He hid behind an ore car, fell down on his knees and begged God to please forgive him. He begged for his family and her family to forgive him. And yes, he even begged Christine to please forgive him.

Now maybe you are saying that after what she did to him, he shouldn't have to beg for her forgiveness. Maybe you think it should have been the other way around...

But don't forget that Val loved Chris. I mean he *really* loved her, and even her whoring ways couldn't change that. Think about it.

\*     \*     \*

The rest of that day was the hardest day of his life. He missed his wife. He really did still love her more than anything. At one critical point, just shortly before the end of his work day, he actually picked up the phone, dialed the police, had a friendly business-like female voice answering on the other end of the connection. And then he put the phone down.

Yes! He started to turn himself in. He *wanted* to. To confess his great crime.

It was only when he relived those hellish moments of watching Perry imbedded deeply inside her, and her begging for even more, that he trashed the idea, and went home for the day.

As usual, he parked his car in front of the house, 'cause she parked her Corvette in the garage.

To be positively sure, he did the usual things. Once inside the house, he stopped, stood real still, carefully looked around and sniffed the odors of the house. No one had been there since he had left that morning. To be sure, he checked the house from top to bottom. Everything was just as he had left it.

There were five call attempts on the central answering machine, but no messages. However, the sixth call produced a very hasty, "Chris it's me, pick up the phone!"

Yes, the caller was Perry. He was the one who had placed the previous five calls. Val was careful not to erase anything, 'cause—just like McCormick's unexpected visit—it was all in Val's favor.

Approximately two hours after he came home from work, Val put the next major portion of his survival plan into motion. Slowly and— appearing like he wasn't sure he was doing the right thing—he walked across the street.

Mrs. Powell answered the door on the second chime, and greeted him warmly, her smile not quite hiding some amount of sadness and possibly something else. Oh, he could tell that she had known he was coming. She had only waited for the second chime to throw him off.

He tried to appear like he was coming to her because he had no other options. He even appeared ashamed to be there.

"Mrs. Powell, I hope I'm not disturbing you. I do hate to bother you, but, I'm worried about Chris. Did you happen to see her today? You see… Well, she didn't come home all last night, and it doesn't look like she was home all day. I'm worried, 'cause this is not like her at all."

Mrs. Powell invited him to come in, and she closed the door behind him, all the while listening to what he had to say. And still without answering his questions, she ushered him into her kitchen, where he found that she was not alone.

Mrs. Hoffinan, and Mrs. Ortiz were there having coffee with her. Of course when he walked in, it was written all over their collective faces. They knew the whole story. They insisted that he join them, and there was enough coffee left for him.

So while Mrs. Powell set a place for him, the women engaged in small talk as a preparatory move towards, the "Main Feature."

They were all nice ladies, Mrs. Hoffinan's husband and Mrs. Ortiz's husband worked at the same firm. Mrs. Powell was divorced, still a young woman, and with no children. She lived there all alone, which seemed a bit unusual, because she was kind of pretty. Nowhere in the same league with Chris, of course. Chris was a lot bigger, fuller, with large breasts and all the other things that made her body outstanding. Whereas, Mrs. Powell was a bit on the thin side, with none of the big things to help her out. However, she seemed very nice, very warm and friendly with a good character out front and showing.

"No Mr. Boger I haven't seen her today, not since yesterday when…" she let her voice trail off.

"Oh come on Eleanor, stop hedging," said Mrs. Hoffinan. "Can't you see the poor man is out of his mind with worry? Let's put our cards on the table. Besides, they were arguing when we last saw them."

The three women exchanged glances.

"Okay... Okay, if we all agree, and looks like we *do*, I'll tell Mr. Boger what we know and what we've all seen."

And boy-oh-boy did they have something to tell him. They told him about men coming to his house, and not just Perry. Other men, that he had no idea of.

Those sweet ladies had everything down in their memories... dates, times, descriptions of cars, along with some license plate numbers, all written down.

When Val returned home, he was a lot wiser, and had further proof that—no matter what you do, someone will see you. He wondered if that included him. And at that point in time, he had no reason to believe that he was the *Shadow*.

Once back in his own house, he thought for a few minutes, then went to check if the 'Vette was back. It wasn't. He tried to eat, but the memories of what he had done in the basement robbed his appetite. So he opted for a cold beer, and some more time to think.

He was trying to figure out his next move, when his doorbell solved the problem. It was the police, two uniformed officers, one male and one female. They were very nice, asked to come in and talk to him about his missing wife. His kind neighborly ladies had called the cops and demanded they come talk to him because he was so "distraught."

He realized that this was his first real test. He took his time telling them his story, being particular to speak slowly and— when possible— truthfully. Yes, he told them the truth right up to Chris coming back home. He talked openly about his sorrow and embarrassment when he caught Perry in the saddle, leaving nothing out. 'Cause that was exactly what Perry was going to do.

They asked pointed questions, took notes, went over the details to make sure they had everything right. Before they left, they promised to find and talk with Perry. Because Val didn't know Perry's name or address, it would take a little time, but they would get back with him.

The police didn't tell him that Mrs. Powell had provided them with the license plate number of Perry's car. And they didn't mention that they were going directly to Perry's place after leaving Val. I wonder *why*?

Of course, Perry told them about him getting caught, and about letting Chris off just around the corner from her house. She had let him hang on to the car, 'cause she was only going home to "get a few things, and tell her husband where to get off."

That was the point at which Perry's story was different from Val's. According to Perry, Chris had gone home almost immediately after the confrontation. According to Val, Chris had never come home.

The next day, Val had been home from work only about 20 minutes when his bell rang. This time, it was a rather pretty police officer in plain clothes. She introduced herself as Detective Sergeant Norma Lee, and she informed Val that she had come regarding the investigation of his missing wife, Mrs. Christine Boger. "Had she returned home in the meantime?"

"No."

Lee was a good cop, with a lot of experience on the job. She was intelligent, and she paid close attention to details. Val would have to watch out for her, or she would bring him down.

Of course he had to repeat his story for her, and again he told the truth, right up to the point where Chris had walked in the kitchen door. Sticking as close to the truth as possible made his story simple. It would be difficult to catch him in a lie, because most of his story was true. He had very few lies to keep track of.

Detective Lee didn't have to say it, but Val could tell from her attitude. He was her number one suspect. She informed him of the time period required before a person could be 'officially' declared missing.

She tried to throw Val off guard by slipping in the fact that Perry still had the Corvette, and that Mr. Stafford, (she had close eye contact with Val when she said it) had turned Mrs. Boger's handbag in to the police. As far as they could tell, nothing was missing.

Detective Lee said that Perry had turned in the bag only minutes before she had come to see Val. She pointed out that— under normal circumstances—a woman would *never* go off without her bag, 'cause a woman's handbag was like a part of her.

The handbag with nothing missing, money still in the wallet, shed a different light on the case. It gave the police due cause to consider foul-play.

Four separate times, Detective Lee asked Val if he had seen his wife after she had left the house with Perry. Four separate times, Val answered *no*.

Lee asked if she could look around the house, because it was best to start right away, trying to find a clue as to what had happened.

Val allowed her to look through the house, including the basement. She looked twice at the big band saw, and he could see it was noted in her mind. While she moved through the rooms, she continued asking him questions, some for the second or third time.

"Mr. Boger, I know it was hard for you to actually watch a younger man having sex with your wife. Were you angry enough to hurt her? Could she be lying somewhere injured, and in need of medical attention? If you truthfully told me that you punched her out, or ran her off, it would go easy with you.

"Even if you did her some real damage... in a fit of anger, I'd understand. "It isn't every day, that a man catches another man in bed with his wife."

Val said nothing.

"Mr. Boger did you love your wife? Did you kill her, accidentally, or in a fit of anger?" Lee asked those questions one right behind the other, after trying to put him into a mood of trusting her, and thinking that she was trying to help him. That she was on his side; it was just between him, her, and the hot water boiler.

Detective Lee was good at her job, but Val was just a little better at surviving.

Again and most truthfully he answered her questions. "Yes I *do* love my wife." He was most careful to put the words in the present tense. Not to say that he *had* loved her. He caught Lee's use of the word "did" and, he wasn't going to fall into her little word trap.

Lee took a recent photo of Chris, checked the garage, said she had to go, but she would return. When she left, she went directly across the street to Mrs. Powell's house.

Thus began the game of Cat and Mouse. Of course, Val was the mouse.

It stood to reason that detective Lee would feel the way she did. In her mind, 'the husband did it.' Which all went to confirm Val's decision not to report the accident that had killed Chris. Getting rid of her body had been the only real option available to him. Had he called 911, the second the emergency team saw Chris's body, Val would have automatically become the man who murdered his poor wife. He would have been judged guilty by everyone. No one would have believed that Chris's death had been an accident.

Val was sure that Detective Lee would go back to talk with Perry the next day, and she did just that. Lee also showed up at Val's job, talking to the foreman, and generally poking around.

She did not say anything to him, however, she did tell Jim McCormick that she had talked with Mr. Stafford before coming to the steel mill. So Val had her pretty much figured, and he thought he could get in front of her, figuratively speaking.

When he arrived home that day, the cops were all over his place. Detective Lee presented him with the search warrant. Of course it was okay, because Val had nothing to hide.

One of the police officers on the search team, requested that Val come to the basement and disassemble his band saw for them. He did. The saw blade and other related parts would be taken to the police lab, or to the FBI labs for testing. Val had been expecting that from the second Lee had spotted the band saw.

They took his place apart, and he was surprised and fearful when they brought the dogs in. That was something that he had failed to take into consideration.

Yes the dogs picked up the scent of blood and of death in the house. They followed the trail to the basement, out the back door to the garage, and back to Val's car. They were very excited when the trunk was opened, and also when they were allowed into the front of the car. Yes, his car was promptly impounded!

"We went shopping just the day before Chris disappeared, and she arranged our groceries in the trunk of the car while I returned the shopping cart."

Lee was quiet, thinking.

Val was also quiet, thinking that it wasn't out of the ordinary for his wife's scent to be inside one of their two family cars. If the labs failed to come up with blood, or the likes he would be Ok. It was some time before the police left, and he could read it on Lee's face... They didn't have a clue. She was pinning all her hopes on the band saw and the car.

Two days later, he had to take off from work to go to Detective Lee's office. He just happened to see that Perry was also there. Once again, it showed on Lee's face, the saw and the car were clean. She readily admitted it. Val would be allowed to drive his car home. The saw blade and related parts were on the front seat.

There were two officers in the interview room with him, plus a recorder. He was read his rights, and asked if he wanted legal counsel. The police explained in detail what was about to happen. Val waived legal counsel at that point.

"Mr. Boger, you are not being charged at this time. Do you understand?"

He did.

"Sir, we have reason to believe that your wife may have met with foul play. Mr. Stafford signed a statement that you threatened to kill both him and your wife when you caught them having sex. He also stated that you forced him at gun point to take your wife with him when he left the house, but he let her out of the car near the corner, at her request.

"Mr. Stafford stated that you held a shotgun on them, but allowed him and your wife to leave. We have taken your shotgun as evidence, as I'm sure you are aware. Although you didn't shoot your wife or Mr. Stafford, he believes that you killed her after she returned home, and then hid the body.

"Is that what happened, Mr. Boger? Did you kill your wife and hide the body?"

Val shook his head. "No! I did *not* kill my wife, and I did not hide her body."

Of course, you and I know that he gave a true answer. He *didn't* kill his wife, and he didn't '*hide*' her body.

He even requested a lie detector test, knowing that the results were not admissible in a court of law. He was relieved to see that his request impressed Detective Lee.

He was requested to give a full, signed statement. He did. It was clear that he had been extremely lucky. Someone was smiling on him.

No, Val Boger was not so smart that he was able to completely fool the cops. He was just another average working

Joe, trying to survive. And I hasten to add, up to that point in time, he was doing one hell of a good job at it.

During the course of the interview at Detective Lee's office, Val saw Christine's handbag, and some of her undergarments clearly marked "taken from Mr. Stafford's apartment." The collection of lurid photos were also in tagged plastic bags.

It took the better part of the day, with Lee working her magic, but Val stayed ahead of her. After which they left him setting in a room all alone.

Later, they provided the opportunity for him to come face to face with Perry. However, they didn't get the reaction from him that they were hoping for.

Finally! "Mr. Boger you are free to go home. Please don't leave town during our ongoing investigation. Your wife will be declared *missing*. If she is not found in the required official amount of time, well... I'll be in contact with you."

Detective Lee had a somber attitude towards Val. It was very clear that she thought he murdered his wife, and she wouldn't let it go. Like I said, she was a good cop.

However, she was up against a clear matter of the law. There was no evidence of foul play, no murder weapon, no witnesses, nothing. The shotgun was clean, and no other possible weapons in the house or at his job showed any indications of blood, skin tissue, or anything else incriminating.

Most importantly, there was no body. No *corpus delicti*! And therefore, no matter what the police suspected, it would be difficult for them to prove that any crime had been committed. It's hard to convict someone of murder if you can't even produce evidence that the "victim" is dead.

Now you and I know that it was impossible for them to have a corpus delicti, because the body of Val's cheating wife no longer existed.

So he left the police station, got into his car and drove home.

The cops did hold onto Perry, for as long as they could legally detain him. Then, they had to let him go too.

The incident provided Perry with a wakeup call. He wouldn't soon be caught in bed with another man's wife.

Once the dust cleared, Val gave it a lot of serious thought. There was no way around it, because he was a good man. He had to go home to Nebraska, to his wife's parents, face to face, and tell them. So he took a flight home, and went directly to their house.

He couldn't hold back the tears of sorrow, and of great shame. Of course he had already called them to say that Chris, their daughter was missing, before coming to tell them, face to face.

When he was looking her mother and father in the eye, it was a different story. He was far from being up to it. The only thing he had to hold onto was the fact that he hadn't murdered Chris. Her death had been an accident. He had cremated her remains, but he hadn't actually killed her.

But that fact couldn't hold him up. He broke down and tried to tell her mother and father the truth—what had happened after Chris came back home, into the kitchen.

Before he could explain, her mother and her father stopped him. They tearfully said, "Val we've kept it a secret long enough from you. Oh dear Lord, we should have told you long ago, but Chris is our daughter... Truth is, she often called home and wrote letters. Son, she didn't love you anymore—if she ever *did* love you. Chris had a lot of men friends, even when you all were here on the farm. She told me on the phone and wrote it in letters that she was in love with a man called Perry. Said she was carrying his child, she was planning to run away from you, to go somewhere you would never find them.

"She said that you were a good man, good to her, but not what she wanted. She said that only Perry could make her happy. She was going to clean you out and run. We tried to talk her out of it, or at least to be a woman, and tell you how she felt, but...

"Val, we're real sorry for keeping it a secret from you. Sometimes it's too hard to tell the truth. We couldn't tell you. Chris was our daughter. It was... a *secret*."

Val had to cry some more, because he couldn't tell her parents his secret, after they told him theirs. 'Cause his secret would only add to their miseries, and he couldn't do that.

Would you believe it? Even his own mother, father, family, and friends knew about Chris, that she was always like a female dog in heat. They admitted at that time, perhaps it only was the Reverend who hadn't slept with Chris, and that was simply because the Rev was too damn old. Other than that, Chris had gone through all the men in the county and even as far as Omaha.

Like I said, the poor husband was always the last person to know.

Everyone was good to Val, and unloading secrets upon secrets, most of them admitting that it felt good to finally tell the truth.

When Val returned home, he was no longer sure he would follow his dream and return to the farm. There were too many memories. And there were too many memories in his big city house... Every time he came close to their bed, he saw Chris and Perry banging away.

He put her 'Vette in the garage and left it sit.

He spent as much time at the job as he could. The weekends were the hardest. One night, he brought a girl home, but couldn't do what he wanted to do.

Time passed.

And just like he expected, one afternoon, Detective Sergeant Lee came to see him. When he opened the door for her, he noticed that Mrs. Powell was observing them.

He and the Detective exchanged greetings. Val invited her to sit down, and she went straight to the heart of the matter.

"Mr. Boger, I believe that you killed your wife and disposed of her body. I think you took her body to the steel plant, and disposed of it there. I think the remains of your wife went into one of the crucibles of molten metal.

She looked at him intently. "No, there's no way I can prove my theory. There were no usable human evidence in the slag, or anywhere else. The hoppers, chutes, and conveyers didn't yield up any secrets. You were not seen, and that was a rare one indeed.

"Oh, I thought of Mr. Stafford as a suspect, but you see he's all muscle, even between the ears. He's not capable of thinking far enough ahead to get away with murder. Mostly he is just a harmless, mindless dildo.

"But *you*, Mr. Boger, under normal circumstances are a good man. Otherwise you would have blown both them away in bed. You still love her, even today. Right now. I think you killed her in a fit of rage, lost your mind temporarily, then found it in time to get rid of her body. I salute you, because you and I both know that I don't have a case. I'm talking to you, not in my official capacity, but as one citizen to another. You killed your wife.

"So officially, your unfaithful wife is declared *missing*. Later, that will change to *presumed dead*. Oh, I'll be around, just in case you slip up, or there is new evidence. There is no such thing as the perfect crime."

Lee was ready to leave. Before she did, she had a final closing remark for Val. "If you're going to laugh, go ahead. Perhaps later, I'll have the *last* laugh."

After detective Lee was long gone, Val sat thinking. No! It was certainly not a victory for him. He had no reason to shout, to plan on writing a book titled '*I Committed the Perfect Crime.*' And he sure as hell didn't have any reasons to laugh. Not first. Not last. Not at all.

*      *      *

Saturday morning, he finished breakfast and was feeling really lonely. He missed Chris, and wished with all his heart that the whole thing had never happened. At about that time, his doorbell rang.

He had an unexpected visitor in the person of Mrs. Powell. She had a very expensive camera with her, with a powerful telephoto lens, and something else in a packet.

He presumed that she was coming to him for instructions on how to use the camera, or maybe it was broken. In any case he looked forward to the challenge.

It was his turn to serve coffee. They sat at his kitchen table, drinking coffee, while she said something about how good he was at fixing things.

Val knew the complementary remarks were only her opening gambit. When she came to the bottom line, this is what that nice lady had to say...

"Mr. Boger... May I call you Val? It will make it easier to say what I have to say. And I'll be real happy if you will call me Eleanor."

Val agreed, and was a bit taken with her. Maybe she was as lonely as he was, and only wanted someone to talk to.

"Val, for a long time I've watched you. And over time, I came to like you a whole lot. I often wished your wife dead, even thought of doing the job myself. In plain terms, she was a slut of the worst kind. Now Val, I want you to listen without interruptions. When I'm finished, you can have your say, okay?"

Again, Val agreed with her.

"My dear Val, I've come to the point that I really do love you with all my heart. Oh, I know that I'm not as beautiful and sexy as your wife. But you'll find that I'm as much woman as she was. Even more, and I'm not a slut. I'm a good woman. A woman who loves you, and I'm asking you to marry me. As soon as possible.

"I know your wife is not coming back. I know that you killed her, and what you did with her body, after you cut her into manageable pieces, stuffed them into garbage bags, and loaded those bags into the trunk of your car. I have it all here.

"I brought my camera and these photos to prove to you what I say is true. All I want is for you to marry me, to love and cherish me till death do us part. In turn I will love, obey and honor you as my husband forever. If you agree, I will turn over to you all the photos and negatives for you to do whatever you please with them."

She selected some of the photos and gave them to him. There he was, as plain as day in sharp living color, carrying a plastic bag to his car. There he was, on his knees—on his basement floor, clearly butchering his wife. The photos were so clear, so sharp, so life-like, so positively worth a thousand words.

He couldn't say anything, 'cause he was speechless, looking at the professional quality photos, and at her.

She read his mind. "I majored in photo journalism in college. I was a professional photographer, before I got married, and did some work on the side for divorce lawyers. The camera uses special infrared equipment and film. As you can see, it's a good camera. I'll admit, I don't have photos of you committing the act, but the ones I *do* have...

"There are no other prints. No other negatives. I have everything here for you. No, I'm not trying to blackmail you into marrying me. I am trying with the camera and photos, to make you understand I do truly love you. If you don't want me, you are free to say so, and I'll go.

"She told me how you wanted children, and how she refused you. Well my beloved, I'm still a young woman, young enough to give you all the children that you want. And you will know for sure that *you* are their father. I don't have great big tits, big legs or a big butt, but that doesn't mean that I'm not a real woman, now does it? Again, Val will you marry me?"

"Yes," Val said. "If you will have me, Eleanor, I will marry you. I will love and cherish you till death do us part."

And she rushed around the table to come into his arms. After he kissed her long and passionately, she was laughing. Her happiness and joy were overflowing.

In truth, it was Mrs. Powell who had *the last laugh*.

## THE END

# THE BAG

Mama-Sue (Sue) was on the streets somewhere every day, rain, shine, snow or whatever the weather conditions. Except Sundays, when she went to church and spent some quality time with Sissy. Oh, when the weather was good, Sue would often take Sissy with her. It wasn't like Sissy had to stay home alone all the time.

Sue knew very well the streets and alleys of four of the five Boroughs. It was just like she lived wherever she happened to be, or that she had a street map in her mind, and always knew exactly where she was. She even knew most of the short-cuts, available to her, if for some reason she had to pull a disappearing act.

So it was, that one day up in the Bronx—an area very well known to her—she remembered an old Italian restaurant where they threw away a lot of first-rate food. There, she could dig out an excellent meal for her and Sissy, who wasn't with her that day.

She came to a street that was one block west of the street the restaurant was on. And because it was her usual way of traveling, and she didn't want to go in the front of the place like she was a customer. Certainly not with the bags she always carried. Oh she was a customer rightly enough, but she could only afford the 'Back Alley Menu.' So, she chose to reach the rear of the restaurant by the alley between the two main streets, which would lead her right to the back door and the garbage containers.

Of course she had to always be on the lookout and very cautious, because many times, people—mostly young punks—took away whatever she had. Mostly, they did it out of pure meanness, so she had to always be alert to any danger. Because she lived like an animal, she had long ago developed much the same keen senses as a stray dog or cat.

The alley was lined with lots of garbage containers from the many businesses, shops, and stores on both main streets. When she was about halfway down the alley, Sue had a sudden instinct to be careful. She couldn't see anyone yet, but she felt the presence of other people.

Then she spotted them, at the far end of the alley not too far from the rear of the restaurant. Three men, nicely dressed, standing and talking. There was also a car parked in the alley about mid way, and facing in the direction from which Sue was approaching.

Her first impulse was to turn around and go back the way she had come. But if she didn't get any food from the restaurant, it would be beans again, for her and Sissy.

Maybe the men would leave before she reached them. As she watched them, she realized they were trying not to be seen. She continued approaching, staying in the shadows afforded by the trash containers. She was pretty sure that the men hadn't spotted her, but she was already planning her getaway, just in case they came after her.

Suddenly, at the end of the alley near the restaurant, a big Lincoln Town Car pulled in, also heading in her direction. It stopped only a few feet from the rear doors of the place.

One car was bad enough. Two cars meant that it was time for Sue to postpone her visit to the garbage containers. She would leave and go look somewhere else for food, but first she decided to stay hidden and watch for a while.

You see, Mama-Sue knew very well that the Italian restaurant was a Mafia stronghold. Sometimes the local Don himself held court there. The restaurant was a meeting place, a book joint, and possibly a counting house, or a money collection point.

She'd seen that big Lincoln Town Car before, always with two men—a driver and one passenger. They were *bag men*. They were bringing the money collected from their route to the counting house. A *lot* of money was involved...

Now the term '*bag*' is simply a traditional hold-over from the old days, when the money was collected and transported in a bag: a leather bag, a cloth bag, or a plain old paper bag, but still a bag. Today, they use fancy briefcases, or attaché cases, or whatever, but the old traditional term is still common. Whatever kind of case is used, the money is in the *bag*.

When she looked again, the first three men had mysteriously disappeared. Gone. Out of sight. The two men in the Lincoln sat talking, and not immediately getting out the car.

Sue changed places to stand behind a trash container on wheels, with the bottom maybe 8 or 10 inches off the ground. From her position she could see the car and the men very well. Her eyesight was good, considering her 70 plus years of age. She only needed glasses to read.

Mama-Sue gave serious consideration to packing it all in and getting the hell out of there. She would never be sure why she chose to wait and watch what was going down.

She knew definitely that the two men in the big expensive car were Mafia, and it was unhealthy for her to be peeping on them. She should be moving on, but she held her hidden place in the shadows.

The door on the passenger side of the Lincoln opened, and a big man in a dark suit struggled out and stood, still talking to the driver.

Yes, she recognized him from his pictures in the papers. He was one hundred percent Mafia. Not a Don, but something above the ordinary soldier.

Suddenly, she saw one of the original three men moving toward the rear of the big car, approaching it quickly but stealthily from the street side. The man's head was covered by a black stocking mask. Only his eyes were showing as he sneaked up on the driver's side of the car.

At the same time, the other two men were approaching the passenger's side. The big man was still talking to the driver, and he didn't see them right away.

Sue cursed herself for being a stupid old fool, and staying to watch something that she really didn't want to see. But it was too late for her to get away. She couldn't do no more running, not at her age. She was locked in to bear witness to...

The three fools were hitting a Mafia bag man. Not just *any* old bag man, but possibly the *top* bag man. And they were messing with the largest family in the city.

Clearly those three guys were idiots. They were number one fools, and Sue wasn't a whole lot better off.

Yes! It had to be one hell of a haul. Maybe even a million, but...

Bang! Bang! The first of the three robbers was shot through the door by the driver, and he fell dead. Almost at that same time, one of the other two robbers fired into the car, hitting the driver. The man slumped on the steering wheel, and started the car's horn blowing.

It was all happening so quickly. The Mafia bag man was forced to back against the open car door, while one of the robbers reached in and snatched the bag, taking off towards the parked car.

The bag man was either very brave or very foolish. He attacked the robber with the gun, with sheer strength born of desperation. The big man took the gun away from the robber, and blew the robber away. Shot him at least three times, up real close.

Then the bag man pulled his own gun, a small cannon, and fired at the last surviving robber—the one who was running away with the bag. The bag man's aim was off and he hit the getaway car. The first round took out all the glass. The second hit a tire.

The last robber saw that everything had just turned to shit. Both of his buddies were down for the count, so he changed direction away from the car, and decided to make the half-minute-mile. He ran straight toward the big metal container Sue was hiding behind.

It wouldn't take the big Mafia man long to draw a bead on the running robber, and the robber knew that. So he turned slightly and chanced a wild shot of his own, still running at top speed. His wild shot was his best shot. It hit the big Mafia man right in his massive chest.

Sue actually watched the man's chest and white shirt explode. The big man grunted and fell, reaching out to the car door for some support. His legs gave way, and they twitched on the pavement, like he was dancing.

As he was going down, the bag man squeezed off two last shots. The first one caught the fleeing robber in the back. The heavy slug passed through the man's gut and struck the very container Sue was hiding behind.

The big man's final bullet hit the gas tank of the get-away car, and there was one hell of an explosion. Bits of metal and glass rained down like confetti.

The running robber was almost blown in half. As he fell, he threw the bag towards the trash container. But the bag wasn't a bag at all. It was a rather large aluminum attaché case. It slid along across the pavement of the alley, just barely passing under the garbage container and coming to a halt at Mama-Sue's feet.

What happened next was pure instinct. Sue didn't think about it for even a split second. She made no decision at all. She just reached down, grabbed the handle of the bag, and picked it up.

She peeked around the corner of the metal container. All five men were down. If they weren't all dead, they were well on their way.

The robber's big automatic pistol had followed the bag, and it too was within her reach. She didn't know why, but she grabbed the gun, stuck it into one of her bags, and off she went.

One of the doors in the alley led to the basement of a vacant store, and Sue knew it wasn't locked. She made straight for that door, and when she was safely inside, she shoved the aluminum case into one of her bags.

Still moving quickly, she went out the front entrance of the empty store and headed down the street, back the way from which she had come.

She avoided using the alleys as her main routes home. She even took a bus to cut down on the time she spent out on the street with that bag, and that great automatic.

The first thing she did when once she was safely inside her own apartment, was to hide the bag.

It had been a long time since she had done it last, but she broke out her bottle of J&B, popped a coke, and had a real stiff one. Then she had another. She sat for almost an hour, thinking.

Then she went into the kitchen to scare something up for her and Sissy. When night came, the story was already on the news, complete with moving pictures. The alley was a big mess.

Four of the men were dead. Only the driver survived, but he was still unconscious in intensive care. The big man lived long enough to tell some sort of a tale. He said that he had no idea, why they had been hit. He and his buddy were just stopping to eat, when the three men jumped them.

Sue had no idea why she waited till it was dark before she retrieved the case from its hiding place. Once the shades were drawn and all the locks set on the door, she laid the case on her kitchen table, and sat there looking at it. Then she walked around the table, staring at the case from every angle.

Until her extreme curiosity got the best of her.

It was a beautiful case, lightweight aluminum with shiny steel-looking reinforcements, ribs and corners. It was possible to lock it with either a key or a combination, and possibly both systems.

She remembered seeing in the movies where the case might be rigged to explode if opened by a stranger. So if she opened it, she might blow herself up. But she had to know what was inside the case, and could put it off no longer. So she took Sissy into the living room, behind the sofa, and told her to "Stay!"

It was a beautiful and precise piece of workmanship. When she pushed the first latch release aside, the latch flew up, making a loud metallic snapping sound. The case wasn't locked, and the other latch was just as easy. Sue said a little prayer, and raised the lid.

It was some long moments before she could catch her breath, and breathe right again.

She had to sit down, call Sissy, and just stare at what the good Lord had sent her way. Finally she went over and actually touched the bundles of bills. The bag case was *full* of money!

Neatly stacked bundles with rubber bands around them. On each bundle was a label with what looked like a computer-generated code of numbers and letters. Each label bore someone's initials in free hand, plus a date time arrangement.

There were hundred-dollar bills in every stack, and I mean a *lot* of hundred dollar bills. There were also some fifties, twenties, tens and fives, even some singles.

Mama-Sue wasn't very good at mathematics. Oh, she could damn well count and keep track of the amounts of money that she was accustomed to handling. But she never in all her life seen that much money, and certainly not on her very own kitchen table.

Man, it had to be a whole *lot* there. The case was about 8 inches thick and about 20 inches long. There were three layers of bundles and stacks of bills. American green back dollars.

There was a good chance that the money wasn't marked. The Mafia didn't like traceable cash. It was too easily tracked as criminal evidence.

Of course the Mafia *might* be able to prove it was theirs, but they wouldn't want to do that in a court of law.

Sue counted what was in one of the average size bundles. Five thousand, five hundred and three dollars. "My God, Five thousand dollars!" She whispered to Sissy.

The next bundle she picked up really shook her, 'cause it was composed of only one-hundred dollar bills.

Matter of fact, the entire bottom layer of bundles were brand new notes; all of them were one-hundred dollar bills. All the notes on the bottom row were in that large denomination, and packaged like they were fresh from the U.S. Mint, or a bank.

Each stack of crisp notes were carefully marked with the amount that particular stack contained. Sue wondered if those notes were the end results of the Mafia having their money 'laundered.' She didn't know, but it seemed possible.

The amount of money in the case would account for the three men trying to rip off the Mob. If it had been a normal bag delivery, there wouldn't have been enough money to make it worth the risk. But that was a big buck shipment, and somehow the three robbers must have gotten wind of it. And decided to hit the bank.

Mama-Sue started counting some of the bundles in the first two layers. She tried three times, but she always lost count.

Before she could try again, her telephone rang. It was her best friend Irene. She was lonely and wanted to come over.

Sue said okay, and hung up. She hid the bag and the gun, and put on a pot of coffee.

The next day, the word was out on the street. A reward was being offered for any information regarding the heist. Oh, and it was admitted that a great amount of money was missing.

Mama-Sue went about her normal routine, but she couldn't get it off her mind, and out of her heart. In truth, that money wasn't hers to keep. Four men had killed themselves for it. The man who'd had it last had thrown it at her feet. She wondered if he had seen her standing there.

On the other hand, it didn't really matter. He wasn't going to tell anyone. It was her secret.

Sue remembered finding a wallet once. She had returned it, following the rule of honesty. But in this case, she didn't know who she could return the money to. She couldn't give it back to the dead man. Give it back to the Mafia? No. She had seen too much. They'd probably get rid of her, just to make sure that she could never be used as a witness. If she went to that Italian restaurant and turned that bag in to them, she would be dead within twenty four hours. That would be a damned fool thing to do.

Take it to the police? That would bring pretty much the same result. The word would get back to the Mob in about five minutes. Then, the Mafia would be after her because she had given their money to the cops. Again, a damned fool thing to do.

She had taken the case on pure impulse, and now she couldn't think of any way to give it back.

What would *you* do if you were Mama-Sue?

Weeks passed. In that time, she didn't even count the money in the aluminum case. She only hid the bag in a safer place.

Mama-Sue returned to that Italian restaurant in the Bronx on Friday evening, and found some good food in the garbage. She couldn't help but tremble when she saw the bullet mark was still on the container she had hidden behind.

There was a big black mark on the walls and on the ground where the car had exploded. No one paid her any more attention than normal.

She was on her way home, it was a nice day so she had Sissy with her. They were almost to the end of the last long alley, when Sissy growled a warning. A gang of men who had already jumped her twice before, were on her again.

There were seven of them, all past their teens. But still a gang of bums, attacking a defenseless 70-year old lady. They took some of the items she had collected to sell, and threw those items back into the nearest garbage can.

They pushed her around, yelled at her, and told her that she stunk. They called her foul names, taunted her with a lot of racial slurs. Mama-Sue could take that. But when one of them kicked Sissy, Sue flew into them and ran them off.

Mama-Sue knew exactly where they hung-out. It was an old rundown building, waiting for the wrecker's ball. She thought about coming back, and setting the old place on fire. But she was a good Christian. She would let the Good Lord take care of those bums.

She checked on Sissy, and the dog seemed to be okay. Nothing broken. She would be sore, but she could still walk. Mama-Sue didn't let her walk. She carried the very best friend she had in the world all the way back home.

"Those bastards had no right to kick my dog," she whispered. "Not my Sissy." She couldn't let it go.

*     *     *

Saturday morning, she lay in bed, thinking. She didn't believe the bag contained a million dollars, but it contained enough money to change her life for whatever time she had left in this world.

That money was hers, no matter how she had come by it. And—unlike the Mob—she hadn't killed anybody or sold any drugs to get it.

No! It was her money. Hers and Sissy's. And she was going to use it anyway she saw fit.

She got down on her knees and talked to the Lord. "Now God, the way I see it—if you didn't want me to have that money and that big gun, they wouldn't have ended up right against my foot. So let's do it this way... If you don't want me to have it, you just say so, *right now*. Otherwise..."

And she waited patiently, a most reasonable and respectable time, for God's reply.

When He didn't say anything, she smiled and said, "Thank you Lord."

First she and Sissy took a good bath, then she went to get the case, put it under her bed, and fixed a good Mississippi Delta breakfast for her and Sissy.

Once the kitchen was cleaned, and everything put away, she called the nearest veterinarian for an appointment.

After she hung up the phone, she made sure that the blinds were correctly angled. Because she had a basement apartment, there were only the front windows to worry about. The door was securely locked and barred.

She carefully removed all of the money from the case, being very careful to wipe it clean of her fingerprints. Then, she wrapped the aluminum case in one of the large shopping bags from Macy's, and put it into another bag so she could easily carry it.

The money was stacked neatly into an old hat box and placed in plain view, on the top shelf in her closet. Oh, she took about two hundred dollars all in small bills, ones, fives, and tens. Choosing all the old bills, 'cause they were the kind that she would be expected to have. She could even get away with a twenty, but a fifty would probably raise questions.

Into her old shopping bag—the one she normally carried all the time— she put a small collection of items, some of them left over from one of her husbands.

After making sure that Sissy understood her instructions, Mama left her apartment.

Because there was a time factor, she utilized the city transportation systems to reach the place in the Bronx she wanted to visit.

Mama-Sue took all the back routes to the building. If you saw her, you wouldn't recognize her. When she was near the building, she stopped in another old deserted place and changed her appearance. Jeans, a man's jacket, and a baseball cap completed her transformation from an old lady to a *man*.

All seven of the punks were sitting around inside the old condemned building, on the ground level floor. They were drinking beer, smoking grass, and bullshitting.

Sue knew the Chevy convertible parked out front, along with three other cars of the gang, belonged to the leader, the same bastard who had kicked Sissy.

It wasn't hard to drop the aluminum case—still wrapped up—onto the floor behind the driver's seat. Then, she calmly strolled away.

At the nearest payphone, she called the Italian restaurant. "Let me talk to the manager, or someone who is interested in a large aluminum case that disappeared from the alley. 'Cause I know where the case is, right *now!*"

There were a few whispered words, and another voice came on the line. Mama-Sue quickly described the attaché case, and—without stopping—she told the person on the other end where to find it. Then she hung up.

She rushed back to another alley, shucked out of her disguise, and posted herself at a good viewing point. Then, she waited.

It didn't take long. Two cars stopped behind the gang's cars. One man went directly to the Chevy convertible, and removed the wrapped case, tore the bag off it, and held it up so everyone could see it. By that time the gang was outside, quietly looking at the bag, and knowing their shit was in the wind.

Everyone went inside the gang's hideout, except for one Mafia guy who stood guard at the entrance. Everything was real quiet, then suddenly there was a lot of loud screaming. Mama was sure that she recognized one of those loud screams as belonging to the bastard who had kicked Sissy.

Sue smiled to herself. She had gotten rid of the case and taken revenge on that butthole who had kicked her dog. Sort of two birds with one stone. Or one *bag*.

"Vengeance is mine, said the Lord," but Mama-Sue figured it was okay to pitch in and give the Almighty a hand. What with all the other stuff He had to do, it might have been some time before the Lord got around to helping her.

On her way home, Sue stopped in at the deli and the store. She and Sissy were going to have a nice meal, not from someone's garbage can.

After lunch, she hurried Sissy to the vet, showed her money right up front, so there would be no questions asked.

Sissy was given the works, a physical check-up, her past-due shots, teeth cleaned, and toe nails clipped.

Saturday night they watched TV until the late, late show, Then, they went to bed and slept soundly.

No, Sue had no qualms about siccing the Mob on the gang of hoods. Perhaps if they survived the *bag*, the next time they met an old lady, they wouldn't mistreat her, call her names, and kick her dog.

\*     \*     \*

That Sunday at church, Sue put five dollars into the basket, and wondered how she could give the church money without the reverend getting to it first.

She invited her best girlfriend to dinner. She and Irene had been friends since their days at the Cotton Club. Sure they were no longer dancing, but they were still friends.

Sue was thinking real hard about how she could share her new found wealth with Irene. No, she would never tell even Irene about the money. She knew full well that her secret was only secret, as long as she didn't tell anyone.

Mama-Sue had a half gallon of that better-than-the-best J&B, with all the trimmings. Plus, she had a big pot of pinto beans and smoked hocks, with rice and skin bread.

She, Irene, and Sissy did themselves proud. Then they climbed aboard that half gallon of goodness. Irene had to spend the night, 'cause she wasn't able to go home.

Now I know you will find this kind of hard to believe, but I'll still let you in on a little secret... You see, just because Sissy was a dog, that didn't mean that she was above having a little nip now and then, and that time, was a definitely a "then."

Mama separated and organized her money so she could get to it easily. She wouldn't have any trouble spending the small denomination bills, but the hundred dollar bills were a problem.

There was no way it would go unnoticed if a woman living out of garbage containers suddenly had a bank account and enough money to spend. She had to find a way to safely keep her money, and be able to spend it.

That need was amplified one evening after dark when her bell rang. She thought it was Irene 'cause she never had any other visitors, and she opened the door.

He capitalized on her surprise when he pushed into her apartment and quickly closed the door. He told her if she hollered, he would shut her up for good.

He was in his late twenties. She knew him from the neighborhood, knew his grandmother.

"Boy, I know you must be crazy pushing in here like this," she said. "Now *I* made a mistake and *you* made a mistake. We can both walk away from our mistakes. You get the hell out of here, and I'll forget you were here. Deal?"

"Ms. Jones I been watching you," the man said. "You got money saved, and I need some of it. You can give me some and I'll go away. Or you can make me look for it, and *you'll* go away. *Permanently.*"

"Boy, I've known you since you were a baby," Sue said. "Do you mean that you would really kill me? Take my life?"

Yeah, I'd kill you," he said. "You ain't got long no way, so I'd be doin' you a favor. I'd kill Sissy too.

That did it. She knew the bastard was telling the truth. Already folks were noticing her spending a little money, when she was supposed not to have any. But she had no intention of giving it to the bastard standing with his back to her door.

"Okay... Okay," she said. "I've saved a few dollars. It's all that I have."

"Old woman, just shut up and get me all your money," he growled. "*Now!*"

Sue went to her closet, not for her money, but for the big automatic. She figured that it must be one hell of a gun, 'cause it had snorted fire from the top front when its last owner fired it. And when the bullets struck the big guy in the chest..."

She filled her hand with cold steel.

Because he was younger, stronger, and a man, he didn't think that he need pull his stuff, his gun. But maybe it would scare the old lady some more... He had it in his hand when she turned back toward him.

Sue held her gun rock steady, pointed dead at his face.

Somehow, the kid was dead certain that she would take his head off before he could bring his gun up to shoot. How had this easy mark gone wrong so quickly?

"Boy, I'll blow your damn head clean off," Mama-Sue said. "And I'll apologize to your grandma later. Now, I'll say it to you once more... You drop that little shit you're holding on the floor, turn around and get the hell out of here. Or I'll blow your nuts off! Do you understand me?"

His voice was shaky. "Yes'm. Yes'm. I'll do what you say. Only don't kill me."

"Ain't it funny," said Mama-Sue. "You were just telling me how you would kill me *and* my dog. Now all of a sudden, you are asking me not to kill your stupid ass."

She snorted. "Here you are standing *inside* my place, a gun on the floor with your prints on it. If I shoot you dead right now, I'll get a reward."

Ma'am, please, *please* don't shoot me."

"If you *ever* see me again, you better go the other way," she said. "If you *ever* come again to my door, watch out! I'm going to tell your grandma on you, soon as you're out the door. Now... Are you going to leave on your feet? Or are you going to be carried out feet-first?"

He left there running, and not looking back.

Sure, it was better if she dropped him, that way she wouldn't have to face him again. But she didn't need the police nosing around. Besides, she was a respected member of her church. It wouldn't be nice for her to drop a dude in her living room, especially when that dude happened to be the grandson of another member of her church.

She hoped that he wouldn't be fool enough to come back, 'cause if he *did*, then she would have to drop his laundry. Grandmother or not.

\*     \*     \*

She lay in bed thinking. If the kid she ran off had noticed her spending money, then it was for sure that other people had noticed the same thing. It was down to the wire. She needed help. So she lay there thinking of all her children, and which one she could trust.

It came down to her youngest son, Thomas Charles. He was the only one who never missed her birthday or Christmas. He was the only one who offered to have her to come live with him, and he had less than all the others.

Sure it was late, but she called him anyway. He said he'd be at her place as soon as possible.

No, she didn't tell him everything. Just enough for him to know that she was as serious as a heart attack.

He nodded. "Okay Mama, what do you want me to do? Consider it done."

While her plan was being put into motion, Mama-Sue, Sissy, and Irene had some real good times together—eating, drinking and remembering most of the yesterdays.

Mama didn't forget her long time "living associates" either. She went to the deli and bought twenty dollars worth of good cheese, and the food that the roaches seemed to prefer most. Yeah, you guessed it. She put the cheese and other goodies down for the rats and the roaches, so they too could enjoy the money that she had come into.

Thomas Charles moved back home to take care of his mother. And—making sure that everyone knew what he was doing—he opened a bank account for her, and put money into it for his mother to live on. Now don't tell anyone, but you see, the money that went into that account came straight from the bag. You probably already knew that, didn't you?

She also had a safety deposit box, in her name. So all of the money from the bag was safely in the bank, and no one could ever take it away from her.

Thomas told everyone that he didn't want his mama walking the street and eating out of the garbage no more. So when Mama-Sue started staying home, everyone knew why.

Irene moved in, to keep Sue and Sissy company. It was a good arrangement.

Mama-Sue gave some of the money to her son, Thomas, and he went into the computer business.

She refused to move from Harlem, the place she had lived for most of her life. She, the roaches, and the rats had learned to live together.

They knew her secret, and it was safe with them, 'cause they couldn't blab.

Secrets are secrets as long as no one knows what they are.

## THE END

"ONE MORE TIME!"

# OTHER BOOKS BY FRED STEEN

### Bluesman

Based on the author's true-to-life experiences growing up on the cotton plantations of Mississippi, this is the story of a young man with a simple but powerful dream... To play, sing, and preach the blues.

ISBN: 9781857563535

### Black Knight Alfa:
#### The Most Feared Infantry Unit

Sergeant Fred Steen served in Vietnam with the notorious Infantry Rifle Company, *"Black Knight Alfa,"* also known as *"The Dragon Slayers."* Tough, disciplined and unpredictable, they were so feared by their enemies that the Vietcong warned their own soldiers against engaging Black Knight Alfa in combat.

This is a story of war at its toughest, of a special American fighting unit—mean as junkyard dogs—fighting against all odds, and *winning*.

ISBN: 9781857564686

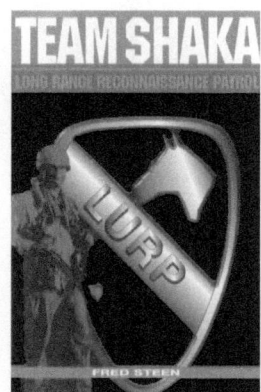

### Team Shaka:
#### Long Range Reconnaissance Patrol

This hard-hitting authentic thriller is based on the true story of the U.S. First Cavalry LURP Team's mission behind enemy lines to break up a plot to distribute several tons of uncut heroin among American soldiers in South Vietnam. According to recently-released CIA documents, those implicated in the plot included the Chinese and Russians, as well as the Vietcong.

ISBN: 9781857564402

You can purchase these books on **www.Navigator-Books.com**.